Love Has No Ending

An M. RéShor Novel

M. RéShor

Published by Different Shades of Writers
Printed in the United States of America
ISBN: 069224767X
ISBN 13: 9780692247679
Library of Congress Control Number: 2014911957
Different Shade of Writers, Beverly Hills, CA
Cover by: Barking Kitty Design

Acknowledgments

To my parents, who are no longer with me in the natural but always in the spirit. They both inspired me—my mother, with her vision and poetic gifts of prose, and my dad, with his encouraging words that I could achieve anything. To my son, David, who gave me purpose and confidence to pursue my dreams. A special dedication to my siblings, Jeff, Joyce, Gretchen, and the late Raymond Theodore, whose chiding me in humor helped to ground me and keep things in their perfect and proper perspective. A special dedication to my darling niece, Lil Joyce, who I lost along this writing journey; I will always cherish her memory in my heart; I know her spirit is with me, constantly rooting for me. And finally, my sisters, my best friends—Kim, Ola, Judith, Gloria, Nkem, Regina, Shirley, Gail, Nilesh, and Naomi—without whose encouraging words, prayers, support, reading, and critiquing my literary work I could never have coined the words and phrases to write this story.

Prelude

LIFE CAN SOMETIMES throw us a curve as we travel its winding road. One day we find peace and serenity, and another the utmost of tumultuous events.

That is what Troy Norton has found—a life of winding roads that he did not want nor ask to travel. His past has once again come to haunt him in the form of obsession. A word, by definition, can take so many forms and have so many different meanings.

Twenty years have passed, and, the peaceful, tranquil, and quiet life that has been protected and safe—a life filled with love and devotion to his charming wife, Jill, and their sixteen-year-old daughter, Madi, is now in jeopardy. The life he has come to know is about to take a disturbing twist, spinning a tumultuous ride of discovery, lies, betrayal, and murder.

An evening of pleasure with the guys will start a tailspin of deceit and one woman's obsession. And here lies the question—is it only her obsession?

Chapter 1

PEACE AND SERENITY

THUNDERING DARK CLOUDS shadow the sky as rain pounds against the Pendergrass Sanitarium sign hanging across a wrought-iron fence. The howling fall wind in Greggs County, Georgia, blows the sign, rocking it back and forth. A rock-paved walkway leads to the front entrance of a well-kept institution, a Southern Antebellum-styled structure. Inside, soft, soothing jazz music wafts through the intercom as visitors, patients, and medical staff move about, mingling. Some patients are dressed in regular clothes; others are in hospital gowns.

Joe, a middle-aged patient dressed in a checkered flannel shirt neatly tucked in his blue jeans, nervously shuffles his feet pacing back and forth alongside the handrail next to a row of windows. Rain streams heavily down the panes. Suffering with autism spectrum disorder, he stops and his blank face stares expressionless out the window, rocking back and forth. Then he returns to his shuffling and pacing and repeatedly mutters, "I can go home today. I can go home today. I can go home today. I can go home today."

Nance, the witty and nonsensical nurse, whose nurturing heart is as big as her full-figured, curvaceous body, pushes a pill cart up to Joe. She says in her deep southern, sarcastic voice, "And what time are you going home, Joe?"

"I-I-I-I-I can go home today. I can go home today. I can go home today."

"You sure can, but first things first, honey." Nance passes Joe a small pill cup and some water. Joe downs the pills, then the water. Drool slides down his chin with each gulp. He gives Nance the empty cup, flipped upside down. "I can go home now. I can go home now. I can go home now."

"Well, if you're going home, sweetheart, better wipe this off." Nance wipes the drool down the sides of his mouth and chin. "Else the female hopefuls will think something's screwy up there."

Joe goes back to his catatonic staring then, nervously pacing back and forth along the handrail muttering, "I can go home today. I can go home today."

Nance pushes the pill cart down the hallway as an audio technician backs out of an office, almost crashing into her cart. She swerves to keep from bumping into him and screams, "Beep beep."

He responds, "G-C traffic." She smiles at him. He shuts the door as he continues to back out. A sign, ERICA PENDERGRASS, MD, PHD, PSYCHIATRY AND NEUROSCIENCE, hangs on the door.

"I guess you're all done, huh?" asks Nance.

"Last one," he responds. "Now, you will have true peace and serenity."

Chapter 2

PRISONER

THE LIGHT ABOVE the door of ROOM 113 flashes on and off. Nance's tablet-size monitor beeps as the light repeatedly flashes, "Room 113 needs assistance."

On the other side of the door, Troy, mid-forties, lies in bed, strapped down at the wrists and ankles. His handsomely rugged and athletically built bare-chested body quivers and makes sudden jerks across the bed. In his unconscious state, his mind travels back in time across the waters, across the Atlantic.

———⊗⊗⊗———

BOMBS EXPLODE AFAR, an atrocity that has become a normalcy in the day-to-day life of this Muslim nation. In a bombed ruin, encased in four cement-slab walls, several masked men wearing keffiyehs stand around watching. Two other masked men hover over Troy's bloody and bruised body strapped to a wooden table. A window with jagged edges, shaped by the many bombings that seem to occur more often than never, overlooks the busy marketplace beneath them.

Clawed indentations track the sides of the wooden plank Troy is strapped to, evidence that it has been commonly used for torture. One of the masked men is brutally rough as he forces Troy's head down, pressing it against the wooden plank so hard that the skin on the back of his head breaks and dots of blood drop on the wood. Troy struggles to break loose. Another man spreads the sides of his mouth open with metal pliers, while a third pours water down his throat, water boarding him. Troy gags and gurgles.

The huge door bursts open. Azra, a bearded Arab with a metal prosthetic right hand and dark-red eye patch covering his right eye, enters. He's angry with the Westerners, tired of their influence on the Muslim culture, and tired of the destruction of his beautiful city caused by the Westerners' trumped-up war efforts in the name of democracy. He's defiant and has waged a personal war against them. Azra whispers to the masked man holding Troy's head still, "Silly American, we'll make him talk." The masked man laughs at what he says. Azra looks deep into Troy's eyes as he leans down to his face. Their eyes meet. His strong accent stumbles through the words as he says, "My men say you don't talk. Don't you want to go home?" Troy coughs up water and spits in Azra's face. Azra grabs a small towel with his prosthetic hand from a side table and wipes his face. Angry, he jabs his pointed metal fingers deep into Troy's right shoulder, leaving a gaping hole that quickly fills with his crimson blood.

Troy screams out in pain. "Ahhhhhhhhhhhhhh!" Blood streams down his shoulder.

Azra leans in close to his face and questions, almost consoling, "Still not talking?"

Troy angrily spills out, "You go to hell."

"More!" Azra demands. "I think our friend here does not understand English."

Azra's comrades resume the water board torture. Troy wrestles with the metal bands gripping his wrists and ankles. His head bobs left and right to elude the near-death water drowning. The glands of his throat swell, causing him to choke.

"Enough!" Azra screams. The men stop. Water spurts out from Troy's mouth as he chokes, gasping for air. His chest heaves.

Azra asks, "Don't you want peace and serenity? Tell me something. Tell me what your spies are doing here."

A bomb blows. A loud crash—the building shakes, and the floor collapses, sending some of the men to their deaths down to a fiery pit below that swallows them whole. Then another bomb's explosion rips the stone wall from its sides, crumbling it to the ground. Bruised and bloody bodies are scattered throughout the remains of the blown-out room. Some of the men are covered with debris and metal pieces of bomb shrapnel stabbing them.

Troy now lies underneath the wooden plank that shields him from the debris and sharp, piercing shrapnel stabbing the topside of the plank. The horrific bomb blast shakes him up. Slowly, he stirs and brings himself to one knee but stumbles and loses his balance, almost sending him down the colossal hole but he is saved. One arm is still strapped in the chained restraint attached to the wooden plank that straddles across a corner of the gaping hole. Another explosion—the building shifts and trembles and dislodges the wooden plank. The plank falls through the opening and rushes down several floors toward the burning fire.

"Peace, serenity, heaven is the other way. Father, I don't want to die like this. Not in hell." Troy looks down at the fire that is about to engulf him. But salvation—a jagged-edged metal beam jutting out from the cracked side wall breaks his fall. The end of the broken chain loops around the beam, smashing his hand against the jagged-edge metal. The sharp jagged edge cuts his hand a little.

"Uhhhh!" he screams. And as the plank slams against the wall, smashing his body, it tears at his arm, almost pulling it out of the socket causing even more grievous pain. His arm is raised high above his head, strapped in the metal chains. Blood travels from his hand down his arm. He hangs on for dear life. "Damn, I'm fucked."

On the top floor above the fire, bloody bodies move about, moaning in pain and agony. Others lie around, dead. Azra's bloody and bruised body cradles the edge of the opening above the fire way below. Fire spurts up the side walls toward him, and smoke rushing up from the burning fills his nostrils. He coughs as he stirs. His eyes open, filled with anger; they capture Troy trying to loosen the grip of the metal chains on his wrist with his free hand. Azra struggles to lift himself up and collapses, but his determination to wreak his vengeance is motivation enough. With great pain, he moans as he slowly lifts himself to his knees. Now, Troy hurries even more trying to free himself.

Fire spurts shoot up from the bottom floor around Troy like darts missing the main target—him. Quickly, he pulls and tugs at the metal chains to break loose then pushes against the plank, swinging back and forth, trying to loosen the grip of the restraint, but with no success. Carefully, he tries to climb on the top edge of the wooden plank, trying not to slip and fall against the stabbing shrapnel on the other side. As he pulls and tries to move, his weight causes the plank to give and drop a few feet more. He lands against a side wall on some crumbled debris that has piled to form a mountain of rocks forming a tall base—saved again from the fire a few floors under him, but not from the painful jolt that pulls his wrist. He cringes, moans, and screams.

"Owwwwwwww!" Gripped with pain, Troy looks around searching for a way to escape. His eyes cut up to Azra. There is much discord between them that runs deep. Their eyes, locked on each other, show the anger and hate they have toward each other.

Azra, determined to stop this Westerner and the pervasive invasion that represents all he abhors, begins to make his way down to Troy, with a knife clenched between his teeth.

Looking at doom from below and above, Troy says, "Must work faster." He twists and pulls at the chains. His wrist has turned black and blue from the tight grip of the metal tearing into his skin.

Azra, now only a few feet away, and a gap in the ledge carved out by the bomb separates him from his Western enemy. He leaps over to the other side of the ledge where the plank braces itself on the rock pile; Troy's wrist is still strapped to it. Azra stabs at Troy, but misses and plunges the knife down. Troy averts his continued jabs, swinging himself back and forth. Fireballs shoot up between Troy and Azra, missing them.

"Too close for comfort," mutters Troy. He headbutts Azra hard, causing him to lose his grip. Azra falls and the knife clenched between his teeth slips down into the fire.

But his fall is broken as he wraps his arms around Troy's feet, hanging on to what maybe the inevitable—death.

He yells up at Troy, "If I go, you go."

Troy replies, "Then let's go to hell."

With relentless fury, Troy stomps Azra's hand several times, trying to free his grip. Another explosion breaks Azra's bond, sending him falling toward the fire.

Troy sails out a side hole and lands on a roof. Another salvation—the force of the explosion ripped the chain from his wrist freeing him. But he bears another wound. Blood seeps from the side of his bloody and banged-up body. He covers the wound with his hand, squeezing, applying a human tourniquet trying to stop the bleeding.

"Ugh! Fucked again."

With much pain, he stumbles to rise. Another horrific blast—the rooftop underneath his feet trembles. He loses his balance, and Troy desperately stumbles across the roof, holding his shoulder and side. Blood travels down his side from the gaping hole. It hurts and reminds him that he was a prisoner of Azra; the blood-filled hole will be a constant relic of survival that he will take with him if he is able to return home.

Stumbling across the roof and looking for a way to escape, he hears whimpering behind him. Troy follows the whimpering sound that takes him back to the edge of the roof. Over the edge, he finds a Muslim woman hanging on for dear life with one hand on a ledge below him and an infant cradled in the other arm. Her fingers tremble as she grips the narrow ledge. The woman screams, "*Sa'edny! Sa'edny!* Help me! Help me!"

Quickly, without a thought of the wounds he bears, he drops to his stomach and tries to reach her, stretching his hand to her.

He yells, "Take my hand. Take my hand!"
She pleads with Troy, again. "*Sa'edny!*"
Realizing that she only speaks her native language, Troy responds, "*Kabbadhtuk. Amsak yadi.* I got you. Grab my hand." He reaches for the woman's hand. The woman cries, "*Tiflaty, ahmel tiflaty.* My baby, take my baby." He stretches more. "C'mon, reach. *Hya, mudd. Amsak yadi.* Grab my hand." The woman lifts the baby toward Troy. He climbs down to the narrow ledge when a sudden KABOOM vibrates the ledge, shaking his balance. Another bomb blows from the bottom of the building, and the jolt causes the woman to slip and let go. The baby cries out, and the woman screams, pleading, "*Ajaara tiflaty! Ajaara tiflaty!* Save my baby!" The building trembles again. The sound of their voices echoes.

THUNDER ROARS AND lightning illuminates the sky. A fierce downpour of rain streams down the window. Troy jolts upward from the bed back at Pendergrass Sanitarium. Sweat drenches his forehead, and his body quivers and shakes as he comes out of his nightmare. Was this a nightmare or something that really happened? Something from his past? His panicky eyes pop wide open as he gasps for air and yells, "Madi!" As quickly as he jolts up, the tight restraints wrapped around his wrists and ankles clamp him down. His eyes search around the room trying to figure out where he is. Fretful, his mind races, wondering what is going on and where is this place that holds him captive?

Troy screams, "What the f—!" He has no clue of his present circumstances.

At the nurses' station, several medical staff workers laugh and talk with each other. Penny, an RN, watches Troy on the room monitor as he frantically tugs and kicks, trying to break loose from the tight restraints pinning him to the bed. She laughs and says to Robby, a male CNA, "One-thirteen is flipping out. Better get down there."

Robby looks on the monitor and watches Nance push her pill cart closer to the patient's room. He says, "Nance has got it covered."

Outside Troy's room, the quiet hallway sleeps. Not a sound can be heard. Nance stops and looks around as if something has caught her ear. She looks at the flashing light above the door of Room 113 and keys in the number "113" on the tablet. The screen changes from a medical history of text to Troy pulling and jerking frantically at the restraints.

"He's flipping out in there. Something must be wrong with him." She pushes toward the door but is distracted by a BOUNCE, BOUNCE, BOUNCE sound that comes from around the corner up the hallway. The sound gets louder and louder as it comes closer and closer from around the corner toward Nance. Nance pushes the cart up to the corner.

BOUNCE, BOUNCE, BOUNCE. The sound echoes around her. As she turns the corner, Nance meets a ten-year-old little girl with pigtails, playing with a small beach ball. Nance pushes the pill cart toward Room 113, and Troy can hear the conversation between her and the little girl.

Inside, Troy wrestles with the restraints holding him down. He yells, "Help! Help!" hoping that someone will hear his cries. But disappointment is all he gets. Nance cannot hear him. Great acoustics at work.

Outside the room the little girl defiantly bounces the ball more, but Nance grabs the ball on its bounce up and puts her finger to her lips. "Shhh!" The little girl, not taking too kindly to Nance's admonition, pouts.

An audio technician finishing his work watches them and comes down the hall. "He can hear you, but you can't hear him," he says to Nance. "Peace and serenity. The work I've done will keep the loud noises of ranting and out-of-control patients in their rooms quiet to you and the other patients. But the piercing decibels will trigger the flashing lights above their doors and your computer monitors and tablets. This is the best work I have ever done."

Inside his room Troy frantically wrestles with the restraints and continues to scream out for help. Little does he know that no one can hear him.

With confidence, the audio technician boasts, "Technology—that's what your screen is for. Your doc paid for some expensive acoustics technology. My best work."

Nance enters Room 113, a plush room with several beautiful floral arrangements placed throughout the room. A long aquarium filled with green plants and medium-sized rocks that form miniature caves sits in a corner. Troy shouts at Nance, "Untie me!" but she ignores his urgent request and continues working from her cart. She preps a tray with a syringe and a small medicine bottle that sits on it. She carries the tray over to Troy's bed table.

"Hurry, get these off me!" He yanks as much as the tight restraints will allow.

She continues to ignore him and fills the syringe with the contents of the small bottle, then injects the solution in the IV tubing. After all, she understands why he is there, which appears unclear to him.

"What! What is this? Troy yanks at the tubing, trying to stop the solution from entering his body through the vein of his arm. Troy yells at Nance, "No, no, no, no, no, stop! Are you blind? Deaf? Didn't you hear me? Get these off me!"

In seconds, the solution crawls through his veins causing his body to experience hard, uncontrollable convulsions. His eyes close, then pop wide open and roll back in his head. He shivers, then breaks into a cold sweat.

Nance braces his shoulders to steady him as he jerks. She looks at the monitor. His vitals show skyrocketing numbers in the danger zone. Systolic, 160, Diastolic, 140. His eyes stare straight out into space as if he had gone into a catatonic state. Nance panics—his reaction is unusual to the medication and not what she expected. The solution should not have raised his blood pressure nor caused the uncontrollable jerks. She is concerned that it might get worse and in her mind questions this abnormal occurrence. *"What's happening?"*

Suddenly, Troy relaxes. His eyes fade closed and the blood pressure is now out of the danger zone, returns to normal. Nance breathes a sigh of relief. "Whew!" She flashes a penlight in each eye, then takes a long breath again and says, "Normal. Sweet dreams. Think about yesterday."

Chapter 3

YESTERDAY

Six Months Ago

TROY SPEEDS AROUND the corner of the bank's underground parking garage in his red convertible sports car with the top down. He skirts into a parking space that reads, "BANK PARKING, RESERVED FOR SR. VP." Sharply dressed in a well-tailored Armani suit, this handsome, suave, and sexy man hops out of the car and rushes into the garage elevator with his briefcase.

"First Floor," echoes.

The elevator doors open. Troy enters with several people already on the elevator. The sound of a sultry professional female voice comes through the lift's intercom. "Doors open, fifth floor." The crowded lobby captures the image of the hustle and bustle of a busy office building. People are moving left and right, hurrying to and from their destinations.

Troy steps out of the elevator along with other people into the artsy-decorated contemporary bank foyer. Local and famous artists' pictures mask the foyer walls.

Well-manicured tall and small floor plants are placed alongside the glass wall of the entrance.

As Troy enters, Mrs. Johnson, his assistant, walks up behind him and swats him on the butt with the stack of papers that she carries in her hand and a small plate with half of a pastry that she has munched on in the other. The wrinkles etched in her face show signs of her age, the late sixties. The southern convert from the north greets him. Although she's worked for the bank over twenty-five years in Georgia, traces of her Boston accent still reside on her palate. Having supported Troy during the last fifteen years, she and he have developed a very comfortable relationship, more fun than work sometimes.

"I'll take the other half," Troy says.

She corrects him in jest and pronounces half the Bostonian way. "Good morning handsome and hand-some, it's pronounced hahlf."

Troy smartly responds, "Why, Mrs. Johnson, naughty teacher. Are you flirting with me?"

And Mrs. Johnson flirts back, "Well, handsome, my darling, I sure am." She winks at him. "You have a nine o'clock, sexy."

Troy leans in behind her ear and takes a long whiff of her perfume. "Ok, gorgeous, you just drive me wild."

Mrs. Johnson laughs. "Mr. Norton, are you flirting with me?"

They smile at each other. Although the small wrinkles show around Mrs. Johnson's mouth and eyes, she's still a good-looking woman. And after all, every woman wants to know that she still has what it takes to capture a man's eye.

When Troy comes back from his meeting, he notices a stylishly dressed woman sitting in a coworker's,

Jeremy, office. Their glass offices are a few stories up and a wide opening that looks down on the first level separates them. Troy only gets a view of the woman's profile as Jeremy concludes their meeting. He reassures the woman that the bank stands behind her and will help get her shop off the ground. She hops up and puts on dark shades that barely hide a small scar on her left cheek. "Great to meet you and this was a good meeting," she says. Jeremy thanks her for doing business with the bank. They shake hands and say goodbye. Jeremy escorts her to the office door, which allows Troy a better glimpse of her. She smiles at Troy. He smiles back.

Mrs. Johnson walks up to Troy with more papers cradled in the crook of her arm. She looks in both of their directions watching them tease each other with their smiles. "Down Rover," she says. "She's basic. What you have at home is much prettier. That one will cause you grief."

THE NEIGHBORHOOD RECREATION center is where Tarleton suburbanites congregate to revel in their recreational activities. Aikido karate is Troy's thirty-nine-year-old wife's, Jill, recreational favorite. Dressed in karate attire, Jill, other women and men sway back and forth in Aikido's fluid motion. The swaying movement of white outfits looks like the billowing peaks of ocean waves rolling across the water, back and forth. Jill's a dark brown beauty, and her color stands out against the white karate outfit that highlights her curvaceous shape. Jill hooks her left foot in her male opponent's side. "Ai yi!" she yells. She throws her opponent over her shoulder, and he lands on the floor mat. She proudly shouts, "Booyah!" Jill quickly brings her palms together under her chin with her fingertips touching the bottom of her chin, saluting her opponent with a traditional bow. Then she assumes the karate stance, readying herself for the next opponent.

Across from the karate room, balls bounce up and down the basketball court, a lure for men and some women players, a mix of all ages—eighteen to forty-five years old, but mostly young. Troy plays with a group of teens and older men. SLAM! Troy dunks the ball. A camera snaps him from a distance but is not visible to Troy.

One of Troy's eighteen-year-old black teammates, Reggie, runs up to Troy and high-fives him. Then another white eighteen-year-old teammate, James, gives him a brother hug and high-fives him. "Game point," he says. "Way to go, old man."

The rest of his teammates rush over to praise and cheer him on for making the winning shot. They're excited, high-fiving and patting Troy on the back, an adrenaline rush for him. After all, he's a mid-forties man who is still holding his own.

The camera inconspicuously continues following Troy from a distance, snapping multiple times.

Minutes later in a sparsely filled gym, an overexerted Troy hobbles to the exit door. Reggie and James, kidding around, laugh and talk with each other. Reggie calls out to Troy as he limps through the doorway. "Yo, Mr. T, you the man."

Troy grins and throws his arm up, waving back at him. "Yeah, I'm the man, all right." He grabs his back as pain shoots up his leg. "Ohhhhh, my back, my leg." He rubs his lower back, hobbling more and grumbles,

"Can't bend over. I betcha they think I'm pimp walking, a white man going limp, limp."

Young Reggie yells out, "Next weekend, yeah, Mr. T?"

Troy throws a hand up and gestures yes with a nod goodbye. He limps out of the gym and murmurs, "Next weekend...I wish. It'll take me a month to recover from this."

Reggie laughs with James, who jokes, "Now that's real old school. Who pimp walks like that anymore?" The two teenagers laugh even more.

Troy limps out of the recreation center up to the curb next to the parking lot where cars are exiting and entering. The camera snaps Troy. However, it is still not visible to him. He walks toward a young hippie flower child, Jasmine, who carries a clipboard with some surveys attached cradled in her arm. As passersby go past her, she approaches them, soliciting their help to complete a survey resting on a clipboard.

"Hey! Fill my survey out." Several passersby blow her off, but Jasmine is persistent. She begs them, "Aw, come on, pretty please. Help me out."

Troy limps up to Jasmine.

"Work out too hard, huh? But I know you're going to help me out, Mr. Norton. I gotta new survey. You gonna help me out, yeah?"

Troy takes the clipboard of surveys from Jasmine and asks, "What's this one all about?"

She responds, "Oh, just the usual, your name, address, occupation, products you like, products you don't like, do you have any pets, exotic or not, future trips planned, airlines most booked...blah, blah, blah."

As Troy finishes the survey, Jill drives up to the curb in their red convertible. She flirtatiously says, "Hop in, handsome."

He brags, "I still got it."

"Got what, your dreams?" Jill teases.

"Animal magnetism." He attempts to quickly hop in the car, but a sharp pain travels from his back up his arm to his right shoulder. An old nagging pain, and today's basketball performance aggravated it. Now, he struggles to climb into the car, moaning, "Oh, oh, oh-h-h-h-h." He squeezes his shoulder and massages it.

Jill chuckles. "Yep, animal magnetism. You still got it, all right."

"Funny, aren't we?"

"I can work your pain right out." Jill suggestively grabs Troy in the crotch.

"I'm hurting."

She fondly tells him that she has skills that won't require him to do a thing—just lie there.

Troy smiles. "I like a woman who takes control."

Chapter 4

SCARED STIFF

LIGHT GRAY WALLS line the Spartan hallway of a top-secret government strategic operations facility that spans acres of grounds. The hallway leads to a scientific computer technology lab. Government funding for this facility has been streamlined tremendously, since the past few years have delivered less and less money for such operations. But this program has been salvageable, and is one of the few departments that was allowed to function because of the major technological advancements in warfare operations against terrorism.

A sign on the door of the cold and dimly lit lab reads, "OFF LIMITS TO UNAUTHORIZED PERSONNEL." Inside, a fluorescent light strip flickers on and off over the working area that accommodates several high-tech computer workstations and wall-to-wall monitors. Except for the computer stations, the room is empty. One workstation has a post-it-note stuck to the monitor screen that reads, "Out of Order." Along with unrepaired equipment and the flickering broken light, it's funding cuts like this that make Peter, a mousy-looking young lab tech, despise his working environment even more.

Inside the lab, Peter stands at a secure door of another room with a laser-paneled security box affixed to it trying to manually break the code to enter. In his haste to get the door opened, his eyeglasses slide down his nose. He straightens the crooked glasses to read some numbers scribbled on a piece of paper. Quickly, he scrambles them in, then places his three fingertips (second, third, and fourth) on the panel laser, anxiously hoping that it worked this time.

The door alarm sounds repetitively. "You are not authorized. You are not authorized. Unmatched body chemistry." As Peter flips the security panel with his middle finger, a lab tech passes by and observes his infuriated behavior.

Peter screams at the security system, "Body chemistry, fuck that. Are you kidding me? I know my finger-prints don't match." Peter kicks the door and smacks the system. "Override! Override—that's what you're supposed to do!"

The lab tech says, "Try nice. Benediction and bless-ing. That might work." The lab tech gestures some mumbo jumbo spiritual ritual raising his right hand with his ring and little fingers touching the palm, while the middle and index fingers remained raised. Then he formed a cross over his heart with the middle and index fingers.

In spite of it sounding a bit off the wall and dubious to Peter, he takes note and blessed the security panel just as the lab tech did, performing the ritual with his hand and fingers, then swiping over the panel with a cross sign. Sheepishly, he scoped the area to see if anyone was watching before placing his palm over the face of the security box—entering a different set of numbers this time written on the other side of the paper.

The door alarm sounds. "Security code override. Enter."

Peter shouts, "Who's your daddy now? I'm the best, brilliant. Open sesame." The sliding door opens.

The lab tech passes by again and observes Peter's success. "Righteous—benediction and blessing," he says.

Outside, stationed a few miles from the mammoth twenty-story glass and brick building's entrance, a row of biometric badge scanner security stalls are lined up across the gated entrance. Each scanner is inside a cement post as tall as the window of a car for easy scanning access and a military guard is on post standing between every third stall. Several drivers pull up, scan their badges, and drive through. Then another car drives up next to a manned stall; inside is the woman from the bank who smiled at Troy and he back at her.

"BEEP." The woman looks down at her watch and the word "OPENED" flashes on the face of her watch.

"Hmmm, breach," she murmurs to herself. She smiles. The face of her watch shows Peter entering through the door. "Now what is he up to?"

She scans her badge, which lasers over her thumbprint. As the fingerprint scans, her picture, work location, job title, and physical description pop up on the monitor.

The guard speaks amiably. "Short-timer. Good morning."

The woman smiles.

He then says, "I guess you won't miss this place."

"Not on your life."

The words "AUTHORIZED, AUTHORIZED" flash across the monitor with a beep. The gate slides open, and she drives through the beautifully manicured and landscaped grounds.

Inside the government facility lab, the door where Peter gained entrance closes behind him. He enters a heavily fogged freezer room that blurs his view. He trembles a little and rubs his arms to warm up from the slight chill. Peter glances at the thermometer on the wall set at 68°F.

As he ventures through the fog-filled room, he tries to fan away the cloudy vapor engulfing him to see where he is going but bumps into a large, clear misty cylinder hanging from a conveyor belt. A metal skeleton partially covered with synthetic skin from the neck down, stands inside it. It frightens him. Then the white eyes of the metal carcass open and scare him even more. He rushes out. The freezer door automatically shuts behind Peter, and the metal carcass closes his eyes.

Somewhat panicky and fretful, Peter says, "So that's her secret." He quickly crosses over to the wall-to-wall computer monitor. "How? Why? Why is she hiding that?"

He attempts to enter a filename several times, but the error message "INVALID PASSWORD" flashes on the screen each time. This was her secret, a project she had been working on alone, not for Peter to know about. Peter anxiously tries to break the password again, again, and again.

"Hurry, hurry, *hurry!* C'mon now, break!" He pounds himself in the head several times as if that pressure might jar his brain to work better and faster. Sixth try, the computer opens to a virtual file drawer.

"Voila, genius. Now, discovery time."

A schematic view of a computerized body slowly twirls around on the screen.

"Impressive."

He feverishly drags and drops file after file from the virtual file drawer, searching, reading, and quickly studying each.

"Juicy."

His cell phone alarm warns him with music and flashes on the screen that he only has five more minutes left before the woman will enter the lab. "Five more and she's here," he mumbles.

The woman pulls up to the employee parking structure and again is stopped. This time it's a striped bar with a metal gate that hangs from the ceiling at the front entrance of the main complex—an added security measure to detain unwanted intruders in case they were to get past the military guards at the first entrance. She scans her badge and waits for the bar to lift. Anxious to get upstairs to her lab office, she impatiently yells at the bar.

"C'mon, c'mon, open!" She looks down at her watch. Five minutes. The bar lifts, and the metal gate automatically rises upward. She drives through.

Like a cat chasing the mouse, Peter quickly reads the specs left to right, dissecting each word to understand the secret behind the secured doors. He raises an eyebrow, and the smile that lines his face signifies intelligent discovery. He knows.

His cell phone alarm rings again, and three minutes past shows on the time. Panic riddles his mind—there's not enough time to discover more. He wants to know the purpose of this creation.

"Damn!" A neophyte at playing the game of espionage, his fingers nervously stumble and quiver as he scampers to quickly shut down the computer. Sweat drops from his forehead and lands on the side of the keyboard. Panicking, Peter perspires profusely over his face. He pulls a handkerchief from his lab coat pocket and wipes his face. Then, he eases out of the room. Confident in his discovery, Peter boastfully smirks. "Secrets no more."

The door slides closed.

A few minutes later, the electrically challenged light flickers on and off, and makes a crackling sound. The continuous crackling spooks Peter as he works on his laptop. "Creepy," he says.

Periodically, he looks over his shoulder at the door but sees nothing. His fingers tremble occasionally as he taps on the keys. After all, the woman certainly is not his favorite person, and it's not like they are bosom working buddies. She is more like a nagging thorn in his side that looks for every opportunity to prick him.

Quietly, the lab door eases open. Prick, the woman stands behind Peter and grips his shoulder. Her touch scares him so much that he hurls unsavory expletives at her.

"What the fuck! Damn it woman, you wanna give me a heart attack?"

She calmly replies, "Jumpy, aren't we? Been up to something?"

Defensive, he responds, "Of course not. What would make you think that?"

"Time."

"If I seem jumpy, then it's only because I'm in this dungeon."

She chuckles. "You're so scary. Guilty conscience."

Resenting her snide remark, Peter shoots a look of disdain at her and snarls back, "You know, you have such a sweet ass of a mouth. This bad lighting and being closed up down here, where anything could happen and no one would know for weeks—yeah, I'm scared. This is horror city, especially with you down here."

Annoyed with him, the woman changes the subject. "Silly. How are my pets?"

Peter eyes the long aquarium alongside the wall. A bug crawls down the aquarium wall to a desert mixture of sand and gravel and miniature rock caves that fill the aquarium. QUICK STRIKE—a white, sharp barbed tail shoots out from the cave entrance, spears the bug, and quickly snatches it inside the cave.

"Well, lunch is served," Peter says.

Time passes, and the woman hides behind the flat-screen monitor working and eating a sandwich. Something captures her eye on the screen and is somewhat startling. She lays down the partially consumed sandwich. What strikes her attention? Confirmation— Peter, caught in the act with his earlier espionage travail coming through the sliding doors of the freezer. Then she sees him sitting at her workstation. She knows that he was able to explore her files, and that does not sit well with her. The woman quickly grabs her purse and trashes the sandwich.

Peter, pleasantly surprised, says, "Leaving so soon?"

She smirks. "I'm a short-timer, remember?"

Peter mutters under his breath, "Thank God."

"What was that? Still scared over there?"

Now Peter flips the script, annoyed with her. "So you're really leaving all of this?"

"Missing me already, huh?"

A moment of reproof, Peter leaps at the opportunity. "Huh, not hardly."

The woman boldly walks up into Peter's face. "You'll miss this love-hate dart game we play with each other." She revels with every opportunity to play this game and dares him with a rough kiss that she smears across his lips. Peter angrily wipes his lips. She smiles and says, "Now your secret's out."

Peter, shocked and puzzled, wonders if somehow she has found out about his earlier snooping escapade.

"You know you love me," she snidely remarks.

Peter is perturbed and wipes his lips even harder; but relieved that perhaps she did not find out about his earlier espionage, especially, since she did not challenge him on it.

NIGHT FALLS AS the long day ends for Peter. The battle with his lab mate was tiresome and frustrating. He enters his apartment. Pondering over the disquieting events of the day, he loosens his tie and pulls his lab coat off, tossing it over a bar chair. He heads for the kitchen and makes some tea to take the edge off and ease his tension.

A few minutes pass, and the microwave beeps. He pulls the cup of hot tea out, dipping the tea bag in and out, thinking and brewing. His mind wanders, asking the question of how he could have worked with someone and never knew about her secret until now, and why was this project so covert. They both worked for an operation that developed and experimented with counter-operative weaponry, so there should have been no secrets.

The front door eases open. It creaks a little. Peter, engrossed in his thoughts, doesn't hear anything and sips his tea. A hand grips his shoulder. Spooked, he jumps and spills a little of the hot brew on him. "Ouchhhh. What the fuck!"

Standing behind him, his girlfriend, Shannon.

"Sorry, sweetheart," she apologizes.

Peter snaps at her. "Is this shoulder grabbing day?"

Understanding, Shannon says, "Oh, you got hit with Ms. It's darts, today, huh?"

Peter vehemently responds, "Worse—she kissed me."

Shannon grabs her purse and heads for the door. "I'll scratch her eyes out."

But Peter intercepts her mad dash to the door. "It's ok, it's ok. I got it covered." He dissuades her fleeting sparring moment and calms her down.

Shannon, puzzled, asks, "Please tell me what are you talking about?"

"Something much better. Her secret? She thinks she's retiring quietly."

"Oh stop with the mystery game and tell me what you're talking about?"

"Just know I'm gonna give my lab mate a retirement from hell." He kisses Shannon's lips sweetly and says, "I love you."

Later, in the wee hours of the night, a silent time of peace and stillness, Peter and Shannon sleep. Their naked shoulders peep from under the sheet. Peter lies on his back snoring, and his head is turned away from Shannon who lies on her stomach. A sudden flinch—she groans and makes a short grunting noise. Her piercing blue eyes pop wide open in agony. Her right arm drops down off the side of the bed, and her eyes stare out in a cold, dead glaze.

The hours pass and the early morning sun shines across Shannon's pale body. Peter awakens. He rolls over to Shannon's side and kisses her naked back. "God, you're cold," he says.

He doesn't notice the inconspicuous movement crawling under the sheet at the foot of the bed that slowly moves upward between Shannon and him.

She doesn't stir. Peter shakes Shannon trying to awaken her, but again, she does not move. She does not flinch. He shakes her more, but rigor mortis has begun. Her body is heavy and stiff.

Peter recognizes the signs of death and becomes frantic, calling out to her. "Shannon! Shannon!"

There is no explanation to what could have caused this.

In seconds, Peter jumps back against the headboard grabbing at his thigh and squeezing it. He flinches as he feels a searing pain traveling through his upper extremity. A victim and a prisoner to his earlier espionage, he pays the price. His head falls over, dead. Drool slides from the corner of his mouth down the side of his chin. His eyes stare out, unseeing.

Chapter 5

Not with my Daughter

Two Months Ago

Troy plays basketball off the garage of his home with Ron, his fifty-two-year-old neighbor and best buddy, on a mildly hot summer day. Beads of sweat roll down Troy's hairy chest. A patchwork of sweat and dirt outline his T-shirt as he gives Ron a good workout. He drives the basketball through the rim with a hard slam dunk and knocks Ron to the ground when he attempts to block his drive. Another play, another slam dunk. Troy bolts past Ron and again drives the basketball through the rim.

"Booyah, all net, baby!" yells an excited Troy.

A grueling workout, Ron lies on the ground with his arms crossed over his face. He groans. "Oohhhh, man, I'm getting too old for this."

Troy reiterates, "You, me."

Jill quickly darts out of the house with a pitcher of ice water and two glasses on a tray.

"Doll, you're a lifesaver," Ron says as he lies on the ground.

"You two looked like you needed a refresher," she says.

Ron sits up to take a glass of water from Jill. Thirsty and needing a cool down, he quickly gulps down half.

Troy replies, "You read me so well."

"Like a book." Jill darts back inside, and Troy yells, "That's why I love you!"

Ron comments as he watched the two of them interact, "Don't take that for granted." Six years have gone by since he lost his wife to cancer. "I think about her all the time. Enjoy every moment that you have with her."

Madi, Troy's sixteen-year-old daughter, walks up with her boyfriend, Rance, who, in addition to his thuggish ways, is obnoxiously immature, arrogant, and rude. Madi greets them.

"Hey, old men."

"Old? You mean prehistoric," Rance laughs. His sagging pants, coupled with his hand cupping Madi's butt cheek, aggravate Troy and Ron. Madi is morphing from a year of rebellious adolescent behavior.

Troy crosses over to Ron and gives him a hand to pull him off the ground.

Ron asks, "Who's the pisshead…her boyfriend?"

Troy, agitated, responds, "Not for long." He screams at Rance, "Son, is your hand broken?"

"C'mon, Pops, stop treating me like a child," Madi says as she slides Rance's hand from her butt and clutches his hand like two sweethearts. She's a bit embarrassed by her father's actions and turns and addresses Ron. "Hey, Unc."

Troy sternly says, "Young lady—Pops! Unc! Really?"

"For someone who's really big on not getting old, you're sure sounding old, Dad. You changed your mind about me going with Uncle Ron and you?"

Troy, annoyed but being a good father, admonishes her about the smart mouth. He's sarcastic and stutters, "I'm...I'm...I'm..." He snaps his fingers in his ear, pretending he's having a hard time remembering.

"I'm old, remember, so I can't hear you."

"C'mon now, your daughter is the star player."

"Was."

"I took the team to state."

"Two years ago."

Troy pondering taps his face, thinking. "Mind lapse, huh. This all happened before you decided to go on this, I wanna be cool act and hang out with the thug. Yeah, your basketball skills are great, but too bad, I can't say the same thing about your taste in friends, present company included. And, young lady, don't forget your academics right now."

"Aw, Dad, have a heart. After all, I'm your little girl."

"Then my little girl had better straighten up."

Rance speaks up, taunting Troy and Ron, ribbing them more about their old age. "C'mon, Madi, let's show these old Gs who needs straightening up."

Rance's behavior infuriates Troy and Ron so much that Ron motions toward Rance.

"It's about time somebody taught the thug some manners, some respect toward his elders." But Troy blocks Ron's path and throws the ball hard into Rance's chest, almost knocking the wind out of him.

"Best three out of four."

"Bring it on," boasts Rance taking the challenge, as he catches his breath from the hard blow to his chest.

Troy bounces the ball several times away from Rance showing off his skills. He mutters, "It's on, all right."

Several hours later, Troy, Ron, Madi, and Rance are immersed in the game after playing several rounds. This is the final game, and Madi and Rance lead with fourteen, which proves to be more transforming for Madi. Troy and Ron trail with thirteen.

Troy goes in for a layup, but Rance blocks Troy's shot and slams the basketball down to the pavement. Madi grabs the ball and charges to the goal.

Troy smiles as he watches his daughter spin in the air, for he knows what she is about to do.

"Watch this," he says to Ron.

"I'm watching. What's she gonna do?"

"What I taught her. Just watch."

As she finishes the spin in the air, she sails down to the goal and slam dunks.

"360° Tomahawk Dunk" Troy calls out to Madi. She smiles at her father and claps her hands, a gesture to show her appreciation for having trained her.

Rance yells, "Booyah, all net, baby! That's my girl." Rance brags on his girlfriend's skills as if he coached her and had a hand in her game-playing strategies and techniques. Credit that only her father deserves because he was her trainer and coach, so Rance's bragging aggravates Troy even more.

Troy spurts out, "Aw, gimme a break. You don't get credit for that."

The ball changes hands to Troy and Ron. Ron sets a layup for Troy, who shoots a sideline three-pointer that ties the game. Both men slap their palms together with excitement. The fervor in Troy ignites to teach this kid, this wannabe thug, some manners. Why his daughter would pick this slime ball for her boyfriend, he'll never understand.

Troy grinds his fist into his palm then slams his fist into his hand at Rance signaling, this is his turf and his game. He boastfully yells, "tie!"

Rance yells right back, "Which is about to change. Don't get too comfortable with that. Short-lived, Pops. Short-lived." He's just about had enough of the thug who he knows is not good enough for his daughter.

The look on Troy's face would make an angel look like the devil. His face turns ten shades red as he barges up to Rance. "Short-lived, all right!"

"Old man, back up off me!"

Ron and Madi rush over to Troy and pull him away from Rance. Angry, Rance throws the ball to Madi. "Finish this!"

Madi aims from the sideline. She hesitates, rehashing what just happened between her father and Rance in her mind. After all, it was her father who trained and helped to develop her basketball skills. She questions her own convictions wondering what on earth could she have possibly seen in the jerk of a boyfriend, especially when that had not been the example of the man in her life, her father. She had never seen her father show any disrespect toward her mother not even when she was angry and fussy. She never saw him argue back. She contemplates her next action, looks over at her Dad and smiles.

"Finish this. Oh, I'll finish this all right." she says.

Troy nods at Madi. "Make me proud, baby."

Madi glances at her father, then suddenly charges to the goal for a jump shot, but throws the ball off to

Troy. Rance screams at Madi. Troy catches the ball and charges to the rim, driving into Rance, who attempts to block the shot. Troy slam dunks hard through the rim and shoves Rance, elbowing him in the side as he comes down.

Troy brags, "Did I bring it? Huh? Who's your Daddy now?"

Rance grabs his side and gets up in Madi's face, fussing, "What the hell was that? I oughta kick your ass for that."

Rance's belligerent behavior toward his daughter rattles Troy. Quickly, he races to her aid. "Is that a threat? You wanna kick somebody's ass? Well, let me be the first to kick yours."

Ron adds, "And I'll take seconds, punk."

But Madi gestures a hand brake for Troy and her Uncle Ron to stop. She begins reading Rance his marching papers.

"Let me tell you something. You're not my father, you're not even my boyfriend anymore. 'Cause, number one, you're disrespectful and arrogant."

Troy was never more proud of his daughter and so thankful that she may have finally come to her senses. He gestures praying hands for this transforming moment.

"Number two, my dad's going through MLC—midlife crisis."

And Troy mutters in denial under his breath. "Aw, c'mon now. Just broadcast it all over the world that I'm old. Madi, work with me."

"Ok, Dad, I get the picture." Madi finishes lambasting her now ex-boyfriend. "And number three, I'm a daddy's and an uncle's girl."

Both Troy and Ron chime in together, "Yeah!"

"And if you ever think about touching or threatening me again, remember my dad has first, and Uncle Ron has seconds." Madi struts off.

Troy throws a thumbs up at Madi and smirks at Rance. He gestures a *you're out of here* signal to Rance.

From a distance, a camera snaps the foursome.

Chapter 6

REALITY CHECK

NIGHT FALLS AFTER a long day of trying to prove that MLC does not rule his life. Troy snores while sleeping in a recliner with his legs propped up. The basketball game on the television watches him, and an open yearbook rides his lap facedown.

Being a dutiful wife, Jill brings a tray of sandwiches and a wine bottle over to Troy. She smiles with a little disappointment, thinking, "So much for me on top."

Troy shifts a little to hug a pillow, and the movement causes the college yearbook to slide down his lap. Quickly, Jill puts the tray down and races over to Troy to catch the book before it hits the floor. The sound of her quick reflexes awakens him, and his eyes open. Now alert, he quickly sits up and feels much pain from his quick movement. He moans, feeling the discomfort that shoots up from his right arm to his shoulder.

Jill fusses, "Talk about women going through menopause...you men going through MLC—I don't know what's worse. You're so busy out there trying to prove you're still eighteen. Stop, before you hurt yourself."

Later, Jill leads Troy up the stairs by the hand, heading for their bedroom. She carries the yearbook under her arm. The idea of having a passionate evening of lovemaking with her love looks more hopeful. She tells herself, maybe after a hot shower and a nice massage, he'll rise to the occasion.

They creep past Madi's partially opened door, trying not to disturb her. "Shhhh," Troy says.

Madi calls out to them, "Good night, Mom."

"Good night, sweetheart."

"Good night, Dad."

Troy gestures to Jill to go on to their bedroom, then pokes his head through Madi's door.

Inside, a teenager's haven. Hip-hop and rock band celebrity posters line her walls. A huge life-size sunshine smiley face is stamped on a corner wall. Troy interrupts Madi, who sits at her desk working on her computer.

"Sunshine, still up?"

"Homework."

Troy, pleasantly surprised, responds, "Now that's a welcome change."

Madi hops up and hugs her father tight as her eyes fill with water.

"I'm so sorry, Dad." She humbly apologizes with genuine remorse for a year of antagonistic adolescent behavior.

"For what."

"You know. I'm sorry for my poor behavior this past year, Dad. I know I let Mom and you down. I guess I've been kind of a real pain in the a—"

Troy interrupts her, "Don't go there…"

She quickly modifies her language. "Ok, ok, ok, the derriere."

"Impressive word, Sunshine, very impressive." Troy smiles, pleased.

Madi hugs him again. She says, "Dad, I just want to make Mom and you proud again."

Troy kisses Madi on the forehead and says, "You already have, sweetheart. You already have."

As he turns to leave, he gets a closer look at her laptop screen. "So, what's this homework you're doing that looks more like Facebooking?"

"Oooh, Dad, Facebooking...impressive new word in your vocabulary." Madi chuckles and explains. "We really are using Facebook in the classroom, Dad. See, this is my forensic art teacher, Ms. Crandon." Madi points to a picture of her teacher surrounded by about twenty students in a classroom. "Our assignment, draw a ten-year age progression mockup of a classmate. All the pictures go on Facebook, and then our friends, their friends, relatives, and everybody votes on the best mocked-up picture of what that person might look like ten years from now."

Troy finds all this fascinating. "Who did you sketch?"

"Guess."

"Hmmm." He thinks.

"This is a rough draft. Who do you think this is?" Madi shows Troy the picture on the computer screen. He studies it some more and replies, "Rosie."

Madi, impressed with her own work, says with excitement, "You really think this looks like Rosie in ten years? I'm good, huh?"

"Uh-huh. Learning on Facebook. What's next?" Troy comments wryly.

"You know, Dad, for someone who's a senior VP of a bank, I don't understand your disdain for computers."

"Disdain—another impressive word. But it's called delegating, Sunshine."

"Whatever dad," she smiles.

Madi rides the praise train that her father is on about making a change for the better and seizes the opportunity to ask him if there is any chance of letting her go to the game with Uncle Ron, Jamal, and him. But Troy reminds Madi that while he is impressed, she's still got a lot of making up to do. He kisses her on the head, hugs her tight, and bids her good night.

An hour or so later, Troy gets out of the shower and wraps a towel around his buffed body, but not before he admires his six-pack torso while standing in the bathroom mirror.

"Not bad for a prehistoric old dude," he says. "Especially for someone supposedly going through a midlife crisis." Then reality sets in, and he feverishly digs through his hair, plucking out the gray strands.

He finishes drying himself off as he walks toward the bed, strutting like a proud lion, showing off his fine physique in front of his lioness, Jill. He flexes his muscles, modeling in front of her as she sits in bed flipping through the yearbook pages studying the pictures. She ignores him but her eyes do glance over admirably at the firm pumped up butt he still has. MLC has not confiscated everything.

Troy playfully dives across her lap, causing the yearbook to shift and slide down onto the bed. "I think our little girl's back," he says.

"And it's about time," Jill announces. "Do you really have to go?"

Troy reminds her that he didn't pick the prize, but it picked him. It's just part of the perks of being a vice president. Jill sulks and about right now is not so happy with the pro basketball all-star game, because it's taking her lover and husband away. Troy offers her the opportunity to go with him and his fellas, but she understands and concedes. "Ok, have your testosterone-bonding weekend without me. Sometimes men need their time together." She leans over and pecks him on the lips with a quick kiss.

He positions his head on her lap. As she twists and runs her fingers through his curly locks, she finds a gray hair. "Missed one."

Troy quickly sits up. "Where!" Before he jumps up, Jill plucks it out to allay his concerns. She laughs at his occasional infantile male vanity what she terms, "male manopause". Jill says, "Cool that manopause off."

She returns to looking at the gorgeous females pictured with him in his college yearbook. Some are cheerleaders. She reads the goodwill and farewell notes written by friends, others and admirers.

"Before I transferred to Filmore U, which one was yours?" she asks.

Teasing, his spider fingers point to several pictures. Then he slaps the book shut and pulls her underneath him. "You don't get off that easy." Jill opens the book. "So, which one?"

Troy ignores her questioning and kisses her nose, then slides his tongue through her soft full lips parting them for his deep pleasure. A kiss made in heaven. He comes up for air and says, "You were. You were the one."

"Uhn, uhn, uhn. A sweet diversion, but you were a star basketball player, and you could have had any woman that you wanted."

Troy responds, "Until you came along, there just wasn't anyone special. Why are we having this conversation?"

"So you were a player…"

"No, it just means I hadn't met anyone special. Besides, who had time? They called us TSTB."

"What?"

"Too Swift To Beat. That's what they called us. Remember, we took the national college basketball championship for four straight years."

Jill flips Troy over and seductively crawls on top of him. "Of course, TSTB was the team's motto. My question again, my darling—which one was yours? I know before I came along, women were probably throwing themselves at you."

Troy reassuringly reminds her, "But who did I marry?"

"Moi."

"And who have I come home to for the last twenty years?"

"Moi."

Troy adds, "That's all that matters. You must be going through early menopause or something."

"How do you figure that?"

Troy wraps his arms around Jill. "Cause that would explain your insecurity after all this time." He pulls her down to his lips, kissing her softly and squeezing her tight. "So stop, please, ok?"

Jill kisses his lips gently and passionately. She whispers in his ear, "Coffee or chocolate?"

Troy flips Jill under him again and smiles, "Chocolate, but I love coffee, too."

Her chocolate brown curves wrapped in the arms of his creamy vanilla body makes a beautiful swirl of erotic and lustful lovemaking. Then, Jill comes up for air to slide her tongue between his lips, pressing her lips tenderly against his, kissing him with all of her passion. She is heavily aroused and seductively proceeds downward on him.

Through the window, the camera snaps at a distance, capturing images of the two making love like there is no end to passion. SNAP.

———— ∞ ————

A COUPLE OF hours have passed. The digital clock sitting next to the bed on the nightstand changes to 1:00 a.m., and Troy lies in bed staring at Jill, who's asleep next to him. He thinks to himself how peaceful she looks lying there. He smiles at her, looking at her beauty, the woman that he so dearly loves. She stirs in her sleep and rests her head on his arm, never awakening, secure in knowing that she's loved, protected, and safe.

Troy eases out of bed and places a pillow beside her to take his place. She hugs the pillow and cuddles up to it.

Troy slides on a pair of jeans and a tee shirt that he gets out of a clothes basket in the utility room. He grabs the keys hanging on the wall leading to the garage, hops in the car, and drives off. It's a quiet night, and he drums the steering wheel as he listens to a famous musician's song on the radio. He sings the words along with the music wafting from the radio, "I can feel it..."

He drives a bit to the next town, not upscale, but not necessarily a rough area—more like middle class blue collar and professional. Alone on the dark street, he stops at a red traffic light on a corner; on the opposite side is an all night retail store. The light turns green, but he hesitates for a few minutes before driving off thinking about the day with Madi and the evening with Jill. He smiles thinking to himself how lucky he is to have and love two wonderful females.

After driving a bit, he finds himself lost. It's getting late and forty minutes have passed. He taps the steering wheel to the music as he hums the tune, searching for the direction to go. He comes to a stop sign and looks down one end and the other. "Eenie meenie...where do I go?" He uses the GPS for directions and heads left, where a few night-life businesses, a diner where the marquis flashes on and off, "Open 24 Hrs" and a billiards sports bar are open.

He enters the billiards club and scopes the dimly lit surroundings and notices a few couples sitting in booths snuggling and some just having casual conversation, laughing and talking. The same song he was listening to in the car plays from a nostalgic jukebox. Behind the bar hangs a huge sign that reads, "Franky's Billiards." He sits down and the bartender approaches him.

"What's your poison?"

Troy's ears perk up as they travel to the smashing sound of pool table balls hitting each other and of course, Rance, still mouthing off.

"Watch this, old man, corner pocket."

Troy answers, "My poison, the short one."

"Talks too much, huh," says the bartender.

"Like diarrhea."

As the bartender hangs some clean long-stemmed glasses on a glass rack he comments, "He comes in here about three to four times a week, hustling, especially drunk old men and talks all kinds of shit." The bartender passes Troy a bottle of beer and says, "Follow the shit."

Troy nods at the bartender and raises his beer bottle at him in agreement that Rance is a true butthead.

"And when you get tired of the shit, remember, I sell liquor." The bartender sets a shot glass of red liquor on the bar in front of Troy and says, "On the house."

Rance is getting the best of a man who looks to be about twenty to thirty years older than him. Poised to shoot the eight ball, Rance takes the shot.

"The sad thing is, he'll back it up," the bartender says, gesturing toward Rance.

The ball sinks into the corner pocket.

"No humility, huh?"

"None," says Troy.

Troy moves closer to the pool table and stands behind a few people so as not to make himself visible to Rance. He studies, watches, and listens to Rance who's obnoxious with his laughing and bragging.

"Who's the best? Me. Pay up, old man."

The old man slaps two fifty-dollar bills down hard on the pool table covering them with his hand and a lingering thought before Rance takes the money. "Manners go a long way, kid."

"You talking to me? Nah…"

Reluctantly, the old man releases the money. Rance grabs the two bills and adds it to the thick roll he already has, but not before humiliating the elderly man even more. He pulls a five-dollar bill out and slides it in the Old Man's shirt pocket. "How about that for manners?"

"Why you little…"

The old man is about to punch Rance but is stopped. Troy intercedes and slides the shot glass of red liquor into the old man's hand instead. The old man swallows it in one gulp and stumbles out.

"Still your same MO," Troy says.

"Look who's here, another old G." Rance tries to insult.

Troy lays a $100 bill on the pool table.

"Me...you. Oh, this won't take long." Rance lays his hundred on top of the money.

The bartender yells, "We close at three."

Rance looks at the clock hanging on the wall and it shows 2:30 a.m. Cocky, he yells back, "I only need fifteen. Rack 'em."

The game begins and the winner takes all. Troy racks the balls then sinks a striped ball in the side pocket.

Fourteen minutes have passed. The bartender rings the last call bell. All of the solid-colored balls are still on the table. Only one striped ball remains, and Troy shoots and sinks it in a corner pocket. He grabs the cue ball. "Eight ball, corner pocket." Then, sinks it. What pleasure he gets in winning the game and beating this arrogant and despicable thug who walks on God's beautiful and bountiful creation, earth. *What a waste*, he thinks in his mind.

Rance is so angry that he slams the pool stick hard on the table several times until he breaks it in half. "Asshole!"

"That'll cost you," yells the bartender.

Rance disregards the bartender's aggravation and storms out of the bar.

Troy pays the bartender a couple of hundred dollars for the broken pool stick. "Will this cover it?"

"Yeah."

⸺∞⸺

A SHORT DISTANCE down the street, Troy is back in his car driving when he sees Rance fussing, cussing, and kicking his car parked on the side of the street. Troy drives up to him with the passenger window down.

"Can this asshole help you?"

"This fucking car..."

"Try something different for a change."

"Different?"

"Be nice."

Rance pounds the hood of the car with his fist, hard, ignoring Troy.

"Hop in, I'll take you home."

"You'd do that?" Rance somewhat surprised is suspicious of Troy's offer to help him.

Troy leans over to the passenger door and opens it. Rance hesitates with some reservation before getting in, wondering if this man is that forgiving. After all, he realizes that he more than got under Troy's skin with their earlier rendezvous. But, unfortunately, his arrogance won't let him stop. He hops into the car.

"Which way do I go?" Troy asks.

Rance points in the direction the car is going and says, "I'm on the other side of town. Just go down this street for about twenty minutes."

Troy cruises down the street and as quickly as they take off, Rance gets comfortable resting his head back on the headrest. He dozes off.

About thirty minutes later, he wakes up. "How long have I been out?"

"Oh, just a little while."

Rance looks around to find himself riding down a lonely two-lane back road in a wooded area. Each side is covered with tall trees and thick brush. "You've gone too far. Turn around."

Troy looks around the area then out the rearview mirror to make sure no one is following them or is around. "You know my daughter is too good for you."

Rance is cocky as he responds. "Man to man, women like bad boys and too bad if your daughter likes this bad boy. Turn around."

Troy turns onto an isolated dirt road.

"Fool, stop the car!" Rance pulls at the door, trying to open it, but Troy has locked the doors. He wrestles with Troy, trying to take control of the steering wheel, but Troy elbows him hard several times in the face and knocks him out.

"Some bad boy you are."

───── ❈ ─────

TROY FINISHES CARVING on the trunk of a tree, "R, Bad Boy, was here." He throws a bloody knife and dirt-covered shovel into a lake behind the wooded area and walks back to the car alone.

Troy returns home and tiptoes back into his bedroom, carrying a huge stuffed teddy bear in his arms that he sits in a chair. He eases back into bed next to Jill with nothing on. For a fortyish man, his chiseled nude body looks quite sexy. He slides the pillow from behind her and cuddles up next to her pulling her closer into his arms. Troy whispers, trying not to disturb the sensually quiet moment, "I love you Jill and promise to love you always, protect and keep you safe forever. No one will separate me from Madi and you. No one will ever hurt you."

Jill scoots her body back into his arms even more feeling his hardness at the base of her back. She says, "Promise."

He kisses the back of her neck and squeezes her. "I promise." They make love into the morning hours.

Chapter 7

THE PRIZE

NEXT MORNING, TROY and Ron pile out of the car with their luggage at the busy airport. Jill comes around to Troy. She hugs and kisses him so sweetly, whispering in his ear. "I'm gonna miss you."

Troy reassures Jill that he's only gone for two days, a weekend and that is why he got Teddy last night. He reminds her that Teddy will protect and look after Madi and her in his absence. "Think of him as my stand-in that will keep your bed warm while I'm gone." They embrace in each other's arms. Jill gets back in the car and waves goodbye with the bear's paw and likewise, Troy and Ron wave back.

FANS POUR INTO the crowded basketball arena, Templeton Center, rushing back to their seats. It's halftime and a big night for the top players representing the East and West pro basketball teams. Excitement fills the air. The game resumes and Troy, Ron, and Jamal, Troy's best friend from his college days, yell when the West team makes a point, changing the score to East 85 and West 83. East Player 10 dribbles the ball down the court and throws the ball toward East Player 22. West Player 11, Philben, a very agile 6'7" shooting guard and star player, intercepts the ball with seven seconds left in the game. He drives the ball back down to half court weaving in and out between players like a gazelle zigzagging across the open range avoiding its predator. He shoots the ball. Silence, fans— East and West, quietly watch the ball as it sails through the air. The ball sinks through the basket clearing the sides.

"All net!" yells Troy. The scoreboard changes for the West to 86. Now the West team leads the East by one point. Troy, Ron, and Jamal leap into the air, yelling and the fans cheering roars throughout the center. High intense cheering and fans jumping up and down vibrates the building.

Troy and Ron excited, slap Jamal across the back, yelling, "Three points!"

The game brings back memories of Troy during his Fillmore U college years. And now, the too-swift-to-beat pair watches history repeat itself. Almost, that was college, and this is the all-star pro basketball game. The scoreboard clock counts down, two seconds left and the game buzzer rings, signaling that the game is over.

"Philben is good. He's good!" Jamal excited states.

Troy agrees. "Good? He's a star. Better than good. He's great!"

About forty-five minutes have passed, and the arena is now empty except for the cleaning crew, a few staff, and security personnel. Troy, Ron, and Jamal sit in the arena awaiting the momentous finale of a fun-filled perfect evening.

Anxious and enthused, an excited Jamal asks, "What's next? What are we waiting for?"

Ron answers, "The prize."

"Man, what are you talking about? What prize?"

Ron, apprehensive about spoiling the surprise, asks Troy if he should tell Jamal. But Troy blurts out the surprise himself.

"Guess what! You're going to meet the one and only Philben."

Jamal, in disbelief, thinks Troy is just joking. Troy reminds him that he is a senior VP and meeting Philben is part of the perks.

A security guard approaches them. "Excuse me, are you ready?"

Troy responds, "Yes."

The security guard escorts the threesome down a lonely stretch of a hallway. Only a few badged employees hang around chatting. They clock out and exit. Jamal, excited like a kid in a candy store, chatters, "Philben, we're gonna meet Philben. Man, we're meeting Philben!"

"Yeah, he only made sixteen assists," Ron brags.

Troy adds, "And averages thirty-five points a game."

Jamal reminisces about Troy during their college days. He brags about how Troy averaged as many assists as Philben. "Man that was you back in the day."

Troy says, "Almost."

"Modest," Jamal teases.

"That was then, and he is now."

The hallway lighting overhead is dim. Some lights are burned out, and as they approach the locker area, a dark silhouette of a man shadows the doorway. None of them can make out the dark shadow.

Ron spots the man and asks, "Hey, is that Philben?"

The man pulls a silencer from behind him, and whoosh, whoosh, whoosh, bullets whisk past Troy's ear. In minutes, what was a fun night with the guys has turned into a hellish nightmare.

Horrified and in shock, Troy looks down at his two friends and the security guard, lying in pools of blood. Red droplets of blood seep from the single red dot centered in each of their foreheads. Suddenly, he feels the cold tip of the silencer's barrel pressing against the back of his head making the hairs on the back of his neck stand. Imminent danger.

Fear races through his mind as he tries to get a handle on what has just happened. A whirlwind of thoughts. Who? Why? His friends are dead.

"Look, if you want money, here." His sudden movement toward his pocket is halted when the man threatens him with the gun.

"Ah, ah, ah. You don't want to end up like your friends. Wave those hands high and turn around slowly."

With the ever-pressing thought burning in his mind that his fate may end in death like his friends, he slowly turns around. As he faces the assailant, shock covers his face. Trembling, the words of fear rattle off his tongue, "No! No! My God, no!"

Standing before him, a synthetic mirror image of himself.

Disturbing uncertainty and unimaginable, fear covers Troy's face. The lookalike hits Troy across the head with the butt of the gun, knocking him out. He collapses in his arms.

Chapter 8

MEMORY—I'M NOT LOSING IT

Present day—Room 113—9:00 p.m.

Troy RELIVES THE turbulent events leading up to his friends' demise. The emotional rollercoaster catapulting him to the scene of his friends lying in a pool of blood are stamped in his mind. His eyes pop open. He yells, "Ron! Jamal! Help!"

The restraints strapping him to the bed tighten their grip as he wrestles with them to break loose. His back arches as he struggles, lifting himself and pulling the restraints. But freedom comes to a very short end. It's nonexistent. The restraints grip him tightly and bring him back down to the bed.

Nance enters and seeing him completely out of control, she rushes over to him. She braces him at the shoulders and tries to calm him, but Troy yells at Nance.

"Let me outta here! Let me outta here! My friends! Where are they? Off me! Get these the hell off me." He stares her down with his deep-brown eyes, and his shrieking tone almost pierces her eardrum. She cringes at the sound.

"Brown eyes, you might as well calm down, 'cause you're not going anywhere."

He yells at her again. "Are you deaf? Get these off me!"

"Brown eyes, screaming gets no positive reaction out of me."

Troy calms down for a minute and allows Nance to guide him back down on the bed. She strokes his forehead to soothe him.

"Sh-sh, sh-sh-sh," she says. "Calm down now. It's gonna be all right."

Troy calmly watches her but quickly returns to his frantic rage. He relives the traumatic events leading up to his confinement. He replays the scene of his friends lying in a pool of blood in his mind. With urgency, he yells, "The police—did you call the police?"

Nance is clueless. What is he talking about? After all, she sees this behavior all the time throughout the sanitarium. So, she humors him and plays along.

He asks, "my friends, Ron and Jamal, do you know where they are?

Nance responds in her sarcastic but pacifying way, "Why, of course, brown eyes."

"Are they safe?"

"Of course."

"Tell me, where are they?"

"Sugar, do I look like the Spanish Inquisition?"

Troy screams at Nance, "Where are they? Tell me!"

And she retorts, "Look, I don't know. I just don't know. I don't know who you're talking about. There's no one else. It's only you!"

He is panic-stricken, and his eyes water. "Oh my God...Dead, they're really dead. The last thing I remember is blood all around. They were lying in it. I thought I was dreaming."

Again, Nance tries to calm him down and is clueless. She tells him that Dr. Pendergrass will be in shortly to see him. She tries to reassure him explaining that the doctor will allay his concerns.

But considering all that has transpired, now the tables have turned and Troy, frantic and distrustful, doesn't know who or what to believe or trust. His fearful eyes race in circles, searching for something to help him escape. But to his dismay, it does not appear that freedom for him is possible. The bonds around his wrists seem to tighten. He asks, "Who the hell is Dr. Pendergrass?"

He is consumed with worry about his wife and daughter's safety and letting them know his whereabouts. Troy urgently spurts out, "My wife... Madi—they're ok? Does she know where I am?"

Nance, befuddled and perplexed, shakes her head no. She asks, "Why would she? There is no wife. You're not married."

Troy screams, "Not married! Twenty years, even I know that. And of course you don't know, 'cause you're lying to me. Look...call three–ten–five–five–five—"

"Sir, I wish I could just give you some magic drug that would ease your mind and make all these hallucinations go away."

"Hallucinating! That's what you think this is." The veins in Troy's arms rise, as does his anger. "The hell I'm not!"

Growing more and more impatient with him she responds, "The doctor said you might hallucinate."

Troy tugs, twists, and squirms even harder. "Hallucinate? I'm not crazy. Why won't you believe me? Look, my wife's name is Jill. I've been married twenty years."

The door creeps open, and Dr. Erica Pendergrass enters. Troy eyes the name tag on her lab coat lapel that reads "ERICA PENDERGRASS, MD, CLINICAL PSYCHIATRIST," and underneath her name, "COMPUTER NEUROSCIENCE."

"Hello," she says.

Before she could take another step, Troy anxiously responds and rattles off, "Dr. Erica Pendergrass, you must be the one who has the power to correct this mistake. This is all wrong. There was a killer. He looked like me, but it wasn't me. I know this sounds unbelievable, but I mean, I don't belong in here."

Erica moves with the stride of a sleek seductive Siamese cat. She crosses over to Troy's bedside and pats him on the shoulder, pacifying him. Calm and controlled, she says, "Erica. Call me Erica, and I'll call you Troy. I know all of this has been hard to absorb, but I'm going to try to make this easy and comfortable for you to understand. You're not going anywhere. You are a sick man, and that's why you're here. But we're going to help you get better, much better."

The room feels as though it is going to cave in on him. The emotional web of helplessness that Erica has spun unleashes a rage in Troy. He shrieks, "You can't keep me here! You can't!"

Erica smiles. "Oh, but I can."

"There's nothing wrong with me. Let me outta here! Let me outta here!" The sounds of the staff and patients outside his room capture his ear. He looks toward the door and yells, hoping someone will come to his rescue.

He screams at the top of his lungs, "Help! Somebody out there, help me!"

Outside Room 113, the nurses chart their notes on their computer tablets and pass meds. The staff and a few patients outside his room move about as if nothing is happening on the other side of the door.

Inside, Troy wonders why no one comes to his rescue. Perfect acoustics. His screams inside don't move the nursing staff or anyone to take note. After all, the best acoustics work has just been completed.

Silence is golden.

Chapter 9

GETTING TO KNOW ME

JILL LIES SOMBERLY in bed. The curves of her body twist the sheets encircling her. She snuggles closer into the arms wrapped around her curvaceous body. An arm wrapped around her stretches open, and the voice of someone awakening resonates. "Uhhhh."

"Sh-sh-sh," she says, "silence is golden. Do you have to go, so soon again?"

Jill follows the rich, manly deep voice and turns to who she thinks is Troy. He says, "It's a workday for me, and honey, you've got to get ready for tonight's big event."

Jill says, "I missed you, darling."

Troy responds, "And I you...I you."

— ∞∞ —

BACK AT PENDERGRASS Sanitarium in Room 113, Nance and Erica are talking in a corner. Troy watches them as he tries to figure out a way to escape. His eyes case the room, looking for something, anything that he can use as an instrument of freedom.

Nance leans into Erica's ear and whispers, "He thinks he's married, just like you said he would."

Troy glances at the small scar on Erica's left cheek, not really noticing it. It triggers something but not enough to jar his memory. Erica follows his eyes looking at her; feeling self-conscious, she palms it to conceal the scar. She thanks Nance for assisting her with Troy and dismisses her. Nance exits.

His frantic eyes follow Erica as she comes around the bed to him. He urgently tells her, "Look, Doctor—Erica—this is really a mistake. My name is Troy—"

Erica interrupts Troy and finishes his sentence. "—Norton, and you're the senior VP of Georgia Federal Bank."

Troy, disquieted by her knowledge of him, is caught by surprise as he listens to her recount his personal details.

"Your wife's name is Jill, and you have a daughter, Madi. Did I miss anything?"

He's disturbed by her account of his personal vitae. "Since you know so much about me, then you know all of this is a mistake."

"Mistake, no," she responds. "That was made twenty years ago."

How could this woman, this stranger, know so much about me when I have no clue about her? Troy thinks. *Who is she? And why has she kidnapped me? Why is she holding me prisoner?*

Erica smiles at Troy.

He does not understand her actions, none of this. This beautiful woman is in actuality a villain, a tiger watching and holding captive its prey—him.

She toys with his mind. "Let's just say being here is for your own good."

"My good. You talk in riddles, and I don't understand. You talk about my wife and Madi as if you've made some deliberate study of them and me. You sound insane." Troy stares at Erica with disdain. "Where are my friends?"

She answers, "Dead, of course. An unfortunate problem."

"Problem? What do you mean?" Troy asks. Again he has confirmation about their demise. His heart collapses, "Dead? No...Why?"

"No, the unfortunate problems are still alive—your wife and daughter."

Outraged at her indignation and fearful of the implication of her statement, Troy screams at her. "Don't you go near them! Don't you hurt them!"

She smiles. "Twenty years, I've waited for you."

Erica flashes back in time to an intimate wedding in a lavishly decorated church filled with mixed arrangements of Cherokee rose garlands and peach blossoms. "I can still smell the clove-like scent of the rose mixed with a hint of peach."

Troy and Jill stood at an altar. He lifted her wedding veil and kissed her passionately. Tears rolled down Erica's cheeks as she sat on a back pew, wearing a wide-brim hat and shades, trying to conceal her pain.

"Twenty years I have planned and plotted how our paths would cross, never to part again. So I watched and waited," she says.

Her mind travels to a hospital pediatric ward where she stared through a glass window watching a young baby. The crib label read, "MADI—PARENTS: TROY AND JILL"

A pediatric nurse walked up to Erica and said, "On the wrong floor, aren't you, Doc?"

She explained that she was visiting the baby of a really good friend.

The nurse said, "Beautiful, isn't she?"

Erica reluctantly responded, "A living doll."

Now, at the nurses' station, Nurse Penny and Robby watch Troy scream and wrestle with the restraints through the room monitor. Robby laughs as he chats about Troy's actions and Penny remarks, "Dr. Pendergrass has it covered." She turns the monitor off of Room 113 to another patient's room.

Troy yells at Erica, "If you hurt my family—"

"—you'll do what?" Erica angrily interrupts.

"What do you want from me?"

She responds, "I want that fallacy of a marriage to end. I want what should have been mine."

He is aghast at the thought of them together. He loathes the very idea and has no clue what could have ever led her to think that something existed between them. "I don't know you."

"Well, let me tell you a love story," Erica declares. "Once upon a time, we met."

"Where?"

"You were a star basketball player."

"Fillmore." His mind goes back in time to his college days. The place where Jill and he met. But he does not recall ever seeing Erica, whose obsessive infatuation has driven her to this unimaginable plot.

Erica went on. "I loved our Psych 401 class. Every Tuesday and Thursday, we would see each other."

Unaware of how she conjured up the idea that anything existed between them, Troy states, "See each other? We didn't have any classes together, and if we did, then you would know it was always Jill."

"Don't say that! Don't say that. You didn't want her. You wanted me!" she shouts. She abhors his love for Jill and loses her control, crying. But quickly dries her tears and dismisses his reaction of devotion to Jill. She acts as if she has not heard a word he said.

Thinking back to those college years, she says, "The class was always full and every seat occupied. If you didn't get in there early, then you would not have choice seating."

"Uh, huh." Troy agrees and is so amazed at her knowledge of a time in his past and did not understand her recollection.

"I always sat at row 6, seven over," she tells him.

Realization starts to hit him. "Tiered seating, right between Jill and me. And I always ran late." Troy had to come from the other side of campus and could never get there early. This being his last semester and a required course, he couldn't reschedule it. "Rarely did I get a seat next to her."

"That's because you sat next to me. I always saved a seat for you. Erica nodded.

"Bird's nest."

"What did you call me?" which offends Erica.

Troy remembers the odd-looking type who always sat alone in the classroom. No one sat next to her— except one day, when he did. He was running late again and it was the only open seat. Jill had tried to save him a seat, but it was a big class and the only class offered that semester for a lot of graduating and close to graduating upper class students.

He felt sorry for Erica sitting there all alone. All of the seats were occupied except the one by Erica. He looked around the room one more time to make sure there were no empties, but didn't find any others except for the seat next to her. And, hiding behind the not-so-fashionable cat glasses that were so uncouth for the nineties, were her sad eyes.

That seem to say, no beg me not to abandon or isolate her as everyone always did. So, out of pity I rescued her from humiliation. I made my way over to the only empty seat next to her.

"Bird's nest" is what the students called her. Her hair was always unkempt, and she wore those funny-looking blue vintage cat eyeglasses. She was not an attractive sort. The students were a bit pretentious and would squeamishly move or just ignore her when Erica passed in front or by them.

Troy says, "You were the one with the creative look."

"Creative. How kind? Not different, not crazy, not..."

"Strange," he muffles.

Erica, angry, retorts, "I know what you said. I know what you all said about me. You thought I was strange, crazy; and maybe I was."

Erica grabs the syringe lying on the medical tray next to Troy's bed. She nervously jabs herself several times in the side stabbing her hip through her lab coat and the pain, due to a habit that has become more prevalent in her life over the years, is almost null. She feels the slight pricks but has become a bit desensitized to emotional and physical pain from the scars she bore as a child. Her father was cruel and nonexistent in her life. And the emotional wounds have followed her even as an adult. "You were kind and I was crazy in love with you. I've never stopped. I know you wanted me." An immature schoolgirl crush, she giggles and convinced herself of a lie.

She cries out in pain when she sticks herself again. Blood seeps through the lab coat. "And don't forget the love letters."

"Love letters? I-I-I never sent you any love letters."

"You drew a heart with the words, 'Our love never ends.'"

Troy vaguely remembers one of the many times that he did not sit next to Erica. He had drawn a heart for Jill, who sat several seats up behind him, and flashed it at her; she smiled at the romantic gesture. Erica sat in their line of view, watching Troy form a heart with his hands that she imagined was for her. Mesmerized and totally obsessed with Troy, she believed he was flashing the picture and saying "I love you" to her. He'd never noticed Erica, never even gave her a glimpse. As students exited at the end of class on that day, it was then that her mind fabricated a love story that never existed on Troy's part.

After class, he waited for Jill at the bottom of the stairs. Troy had stuffed the drawing in his book. Another student rushing past him bumped Troy and knocked his books on the floor.

"Excuse me, man," the student apologizes.

The drawing slid under a seat. Neither Troy nor Jill noticed it as they exited the classroom.

But Erica did. She grabbed the drawing from under the seat, inhaled the paper scent from Troy's touch— imagining her in his arms. She closed her eyes and clutched the paper drawing to her heart, savoring the moment. After all, she had never known a man nor felt the touch of a boyfriend. She only had a crush, a love obsession with someone who only tried to be nice to her and showed her a bit of kindness out of pity.

Erica now cries, "You were my first, and I've never forgotten you."

"First what?" Troy asks.

Erica stands at the foot of the bed. "I know you wanted me, but she was always in the way."

"My wife...in the way of what?" Troy frantically asks. "I don't even know you!"

Erica becomes impatient and agitated with him. She yells. "Stop denying us!" She begins to dig her fingernails into the wood grain of Troy's bed. "I'm not crazy!"

Incredulous, Troy stares at Erica grinding her fingernails deeper into the wood. Small crumbled pieces of the wood fall on the white bed linen.

"I'm not like the nutcases in here who tell me their problems every day or how crazy they are. I'm not crazy! Ummm." She moans and flinches from a painful splinter stuck in her finger from the wood.

"No, you're not crazy." Troy cringes as he watches her fingers dig into the wood.

Erica rambles, "And then, my secret. Peter was gonna tell, but I fixed him." She cups her painful finger in her hand.

"Peter, who is Peter? What did you do? Kill him?"

"What do you think I did? And I'm gonna take care of her, too." Erica squints from the pain.

"If you do anything to hurt my wife or daughter...you think you're crazy? You haven't seen crazy. There is and never has been us. If you go anywhere near my family, I'll kill you." The anger in Troy burns deep. The veins in his arms swell and look as if they're about to pop.

Amused, Erica laughs his threat off. "You didn't mean that." She injects the solution through the port of the intravenous tubing. As the solution enters his body, his eyes close, then suddenly pop open and roll back in his head. He shivers and breaks into a cold sweat shaking more and more, an uncontrollable reaction.

"What is this stuff you keep shooting in my veins?"

"Something to relax you."

"Relax me." His body perspires and shivers profusely. She assures him that what he's experiencing will be over shortly and her behavior becomes more erratic and disturbing.

"She's not your wife. She was just a little toy that you wanted to play with and I understood. I allowed you to have your moment of male sexual indiscretion." Angry and frustrated, Erica adds, "But, then you had a daughter, and that complicated things even more."

Troy, barely able to speak as his body jerks uncontrollably, stutters, "Com-com-com-complicated th-th-th-things?"

Erica sighs. "Plan A didn't work." She scolds him for bringing his friends and shakes her finger at him. "You brought your friends. The two tickets were for your wife and daughter."

Troy's words come out as a groggy stutter, a medically induced reaction, as he tries to scream out, "They would have been killed!"

Erica boasts, "Wasn't it brilliant?"

Troy, in a violent rage, struggles to twist and turn pulling on the restraints. As his body succumbs to the medication, his eyes get heavy. He moves in slow motion and they slowly close. With little fight left to resist the medication taking over his body, he slowly opens them again.

Erica taunts him. "Almost about to fall asleep. Your eyes are getting heavy, huh? Sleep, not yet. I want you to see something." Erica presses her lips to Troy's and he retaliates. He musters enough strength to bite her bottom lip. Blood spurts out. She wipes her lip and smears the blood on Troy's face.

He is so groggy and sluggish. "Y-y-you won't... get away...I-I-I'm missing. The police are looking for me."

Erica exhales an air of confidence. "Police, huh. I'm brilliant. Remember?" She grabs the remote from the desk next to his bed and flips the huge wall-to-wall screen on. "It won't be me who takes your precious family away. It will be you."

Bitterly groggy and not quite understanding, his eyes slowly trail Erica's movements over to the screen. On the screen, Jill steps out of the shower at their home. She wraps a towel around her curves and begins to blow dry her hair. A hand wraps around the back of her neck which startles her. Jill jumps and turns around into the arms of another. Another man.

She shivers. "Cold." Her eyes lovingly gaze into the brown eyes of her love, a Troy lookalike.

"What?" he responds.

"Your hands—they're cold."

The being standing in front of her that she thinks is her husband reassures her that it's not him; but she's feeling the coldness from the winter weather outside. Jill takes his hands and kisses each side.

His computer brain virtually registers, "Body temperature 15°C (59°F), human body shivers. Change to normal: 37.0°C (98.6°F)." His hands warm to normal body temperature.

Anger rips through Troy's heart as he watches this technological incinerator on the screen make love to his wife.

"That's not me. It's not me. What have you done? He's not real?"

"I'm brilliant, remember." Erica says, so very proud of her work.

"What have you done?"

"I created you."

She turns the volume up to torture Troy even more.

The lookalike wraps his arms around Jill. She sensuously intertwines her fingers with his.

"Warmer, your hands are warmer." she smiles.

He dangles a beautiful diamond necklace and clasps it around her neck.

Furious, Troy pounds his bound fist on the bed and screams, "That was my gift to her."

"And, she can't even tell the difference."

"Happy anniversary, darling," says the lookalike.

The towel drops to the floor, and the imposter kisses the top of her breast. He sweeps her naked body off the floor into his arms.

"No more back and shoulder problems, huh?" she says. The screen shows him carrying her back to bed with the physique of a Roman gladiator. He lays her down on their pale-green comforter with a peach blossom design. Gently, he swirls his tongue around her nipple and flicks it back and forth quickly with his tongue as if he was vibrating it. Her heavy pants signal the heated passion of enjoyment she begins to feel. Then, his hand travels down between her legs. He parts her sleek beautiful succulent chocolate legs. "Ohhhhh," she moans with total pleasure as he fingers her sweetness. This begins what will be a long night of lovemaking.

Minutes later, more moaning and heavy breathing of passionate lovemaking resonates in Troy's ear. He recognizes the surroundings, the comforter, and of course the sounds and his protector, Teddy watching.

"Ohhhhhhh…ohhhh…ohhhh…" Jill exhales as she falls back on the comforter, pleased from being filled with love from the man she believes is her husband.

Shock covers his face. Troy shouts at Erica, "What? Who? Who are you? Why?" He desperately seeks answers.

Erica whispers in Troy's ear, "Who am I? I'm a woman in love and Plan B is in action. He will destroy what you love. What stands in our way."

Weakened by the effects of the solution, he tries to scream out. "Off! Off! For the love of God, turn it off!" Troy cannot bear to witness this betrayal. He turns his head away from the screen. It's 10:00pm and his battle fighting off the grogginess has become fruitless. His eyes close shut.

Erica smiles. She relished seeing his anger at the sight of his wife's betrayal.

TIME PASSES AS Troy struggles to break free in his sleep squirming, pulling, and tugging. His eyes pop open, then shut and open like a light flashing on and off. In his sleep, Troy's mind races with fury.

The sound of the clock's metal balls tapping each time the minute hand changes begins to ring in Troy's ear. It's *3:00 a.m.* Beads of sweat cover his face and drip down the sides as he has a nightmare of a rest. The glaring moonlight shines across his frustrated and tortured face. His head sinks deep into the pillow and his eyes open. "I know this is a bad dream, and any minute I'm gonna wake up from this nightmare."

Erica watches him and steps out of the dark shadows. She remarks, "Snapping out of it, huh?" She runs her hand down Troy's arm, stroking up and down, then whispers in his ear. "Twenty years."

He wrestles with the restraints. "You're dead."

"Not me, but she will be."

"If you hurt her, you're dead!"

"Threaten me," Erica taunts him.

"He may look like me, but he'll never be me. Jill will know the difference."

In the silence of the wee hours, the screen pops on to a view of Jill's thighs squeezing the lookalike's sides as she rides the throne of his love.

"You think she will not betray you?" Erica says. "She already has. Remember what day this is."

Jill collapses into the imposter's arms. He smiles and taunts Troy, kissing and loving on Jill. Water wells in Troy's eyes; who feels helpless and the pain of outrage, loss, and betrayal.

But there is nothing he can do.

He pounds his fist on the bed and screams. "Give me back my life!"

Chapter 10

SWEET THANG

THE MORNING SUN shines over Troy's body as he captures a moment of sleep after having a long night and early morning of restlessness from deprived sleep brought on by Erica's torture. He jerks and twitches in his deep REM sleep.

Erica stands over him, watching. She gently runs the back of her hand against his cheek, admiring his handsome, chiseled face. "You are so beautiful, and I am so lucky...you here with me."

His eyes pop open. Standing over him, an earthquake shattering his life and taking his freedom is the master he loathes. She leans in to kiss him. He cringes at her closeness, feeling utter repulsion. Quickly, he snaps his head away from her lips.

"You hate me," she says.

"Infinitely."

The door bursts open, and bubbly Nance barges in, backing up through the door with Troy's medication and food tray. "Rise and shine, my sweet thang."

"Sweet thang," Erica mocks.

Troy is so grateful that Nance came into his room when she did and thinks to himself, *Yes, my sweet thang. She's my angel from heaven who has just stopped a despicable act. I could never give myself to Erica.*

Nance is surprised to see Erica with Troy. "Oh, Dr. Pendergrass, you're making your rounds early."

Troy interrupts. "You've got to help me get out of here. She's kidnapped me! She's gonna kill my family."

Erica cuts her angry and anxious eyes first at Troy, then at Nance, studying her reaction, fearful that she might believe Troy and aid him in his attempt to escape.

But Nance is not persuaded. "Now, now, here we go again. He's a live wire this morning, huh, Dr. Pendergrass?"

Erica smiles with a reassured feeling of calmness that everything is all right. "Yes, he is. So, I'll leave you and sweet thang alone for now. Oh, Nance, step over here for a minute."

Nance follows Erica to the door, and Erica whispers in her ear while Troy tugs and pulls at the restraints trying to free himself. Before leaving out of the door, Erica turns to Troy and says. "Later."

"Die first."

Erica leaves, and Nance comes around to Troy's side.

"You should make nice to Dr. Pendergrass. She is remarkable and has done many things to help people turn their lives around."

"Really, remarkable. A bit archaic, wouldn't you say?

"What?"

"Lobotomies."

"Oh, you're such a joker."

He anxiously tries to convince her that his being there is all a mistake. "What part of I'm being held here against my will do you not understand. She's a master of deceit, a throwback from hell."

"Man, you have a very sordid view of her."

"I don't belong in here." Read my lips. She has kidnapped me."

Nance pays him no attention. "She's not like that."

"Maybe, you're her accomplice."

"Accomplice. Accomplice to what? That would be breaking the law, and besides that's just not who Dr. Pendergrass is."

Erica walks up to the nurses' station, where Nurse Penny and Robby are having a humorous conversation. She plugs a set of earphones wrapped around her neck into the audio port and keys a code on the touch keyboard. The message on the screen reads, "ENTERING THE QUIET ZONE. VOLUME ON." She adjusts the volume to Room 113, turning it up, and begins to listen.

Nurse Penny acknowledges Erica's presence. "Dr. Pendergrass."

"I'm just listening to this patient. Don't mind me."

Nurse Penny suggests, "You should give us the volume code. Must be juicy conversations in there."

"I just don't want to disturb you with his continuous babbling. It can become rather annoying."

Trying to ward off Nance's efforts to feed him, Troy repeatedly turns his head away from the forkfuls of food. Nance admonishes him. "Now, now, you've got to eat."

But he resists. He wishes she would take him seriously and believe that Erica is not the good and honest person she appears to be. He pleads, "She's lying to you. She's replaced me with an imposter who looks like me."

"What an imagination."

"Help me. You've got to help me."

"That's what I'm trying to do. I can't give you this medication on an empty stomach, and believe me you need this to help control your anxiety and hallucinations."

"There's no convincing you, is there?"

"No, and if you don't eat first, trust me, we can get it down you by other means." Nance eyes the IV next to his bed. Then she puts the fork up to his mouth.

Realizing that conceding might work in his favor, he shudders but takes a mouthful.

"Cooperation—that's a good boy, my sweet thang."

Now, in between mouthfuls, Troy tries to win Nance's trust and confidence making small talk. "How long have you been working here?"

"Six years."

"How long have you known Dr. Pendergrass?"

"Six years."

"So you didn't know her before you came here?"

"No, I didn't know her personally, but I knew of her. She's done a lot of important work and is well recognized for her research studies on the benefits of entomology with neuroscience and psychology. She was also a leading consultant for the Defense Department."

"Defense? What did she do? Covert Operations?"

"Well, I don't know about all that, but she pays very well, too."

"So money drives you?"

"Sweet thang, in these days and times, money drives everything. You ask a lot of questions about her, but tell me about your family. Tell me about your wife."

Troy pauses before answering because he's not sure why she asked. She has not shown any interest before. "Jill, that's her name is as beautiful inside as she is on the outside. We would be celebrating our twentieth anniversary in a few weeks. He describes the charity work that she does with the shelter helping women get new starts and away from domestic violence."

"She sounds perfect."

"So, you believe me now."

Erica comes in and interrupts. "How are we doing?"

"Just fine, Dr. Pendergrass. He's just finished eating."

"Good. I'll take over now. You can go."

"But...but, I haven't given him his medication."

"I can do that. Go now."

Nance quickly organizes the food tray and collects her things. She moves with urgency toward the door. But before exiting the room, she blows a kiss to Troy. "Later, sweet thang." She exits.

Erica sarcastically remarks, "Bosom buddies, huh?"

"Jealous," Troy asserts.

"You will come around, one way or another."

Erica stabs Troy in the arm with the syringe that she pulls out of her pocket. His body reacts with the sudden convulsive jerks and tremors. Thunder cries out as violently as the rain starts pouring down the sides of the window. Immediately, Troy becomes groggy.

"I-I-I-I...I-I ha...hat-hate you." His eyes close.

"Not for long, sweet thang. Not for long."

Chapter 11

WHAT DAY IS THIS?

ERICA LOOKS OUT the window, her mood dark and sullen. The clouds are gray with intermittent rain showers. "I hate the rain. It makes me sad." Bolts of lightning flash periodically through the clouds. "Something always happens when it rains to make me sad."

She looks over at Troy who wakes up. His blankless face and eyes stare at her.

"Don't make me sad," she says. Then, she exits.

Troy's mind goes round and round trying to figure out a way to escape as he listened to Erica's threat. While she's gone, he looks around the room, searching for something to help him break loose. Something to relinquish her bonds of savagery. It's 4:00 p.m. He sees no escape.

Erica enters Troy's room again and crosses over to his bed. She gently strokes his forehead and asks, "What have you decided?"

Troy adamantly responds, "I have a wife and a daughter whom I love very much. Nothing changes that."

"Really. That makes me sad. What day is this?"
The wall-to-wall screen pops on.

— ◠◠◠ —

SOOTHING JAZZ MUSIC plays over the intercom of a two-story upscale, contemporary-decorated art gallery. Abstract art hangs throughout different rooms on the walls and from the high, vaulted ceilings. At the entrance, two long rectangular metal sheets hang from the ceiling, each covered with colorful indentations that form abstract pictures of shapely women of different ethnicities. One hanging metal sheet depicts an African woman with child, and another shows a Far East Asian mother cradling a child in her bosom. These women represent the theme of the night, "We May be Different, but We All Share the Same Burden."

Examples of the contemporary abstract deco art drape the staircase sides of the posh affair. Art connoisseurs, critics, and guests are dressed in evening clothes and gather at the entrance of a red carpet event. It's the who's who list of attendees—the mayor and her husband, several city council members, a few members of Congress, movie and music celebrities, and others. Jill and the lookalike of Troy enter with Madi walking a little ahead between them. Jill wears a very seductive low-cut classy dress that clings to every inch of her shapely body while Troy's hand rides her hip as he pulls her close to him. They walk up to a middle-aged, handsome man with salt and pepper hair who is talking to several men and women.

"And there she is, the queen of the night." The man pecks Jill on the cheek. "And you the proud husband."

Troy shakes the man's hand, greeting him. "Senator Ortiz, it's always good to see you." Senator Ortiz responds, "I'll need your support in the coming election. Can I count on you and this beautiful young lady who takes after her mother? I hope you will soon be a voting constituent of mine, too."

"In a few years, Senator Ortiz, in a few years," says Madi. The dimples set in her lovely smile are cute as buttons. She's proud to be the daughter of Jill and the impostor whom she refers to as Dad. She politely responds, "Thank you, Senator Ortiz. But you know my dad had something to do with this, too."

"You're the envy of every man in this room and some women," he says to the impostor. Jill's gorgeous, talented, and thanks to her, we've been able to help many families. A lot of mothers and their children have safe homes, now."

"Yes, she is wonderful and she's mine, all mine."

Troy yells at the screen, "Madi! Madi! He's not me. Sunshine, can't you see? It's not me."

Waiters and waitresses serve the guests throughout the rooms—men in black tuxedoes and women adorned in diamonds and expensive jewelry dressed in lovely, stylish evening gowns. They mingle and socialize with one another admiring the art work and drinking champagne.

He now stands next to Jeremy, talking and sipping champagne. Jeremy compliments him. "You're a lucky man. How many years?"

"Twenty."

"She's a successful artist. Twenty years of blissful marriage with a gorgeous woman. I'm jealous."

"Watch it now." He smiles at Jill across the room on stage as she prepares to give a speech.

Jill smiles back at the man she thinks is her husband; the man who has kept her bed warm and body caressed in love. The lookalike raises his glass to toast and cheer her on. He winks his eye at Jill.

———— ∞ ————

RAIN POUNDS AGAINST the glass as the water streams down the windowpanes at the sanitarium. Lightning flashes through the windows against the sides of the aquarium. Troy looks away from the torture screen for a second. The pain he feels from being separated from his family is unbearable. A tear rolls down the side of his face, but then a stirring sound captures his ear. The sound, a coarse drag travels up and down from one end to another inside the aquarium. But the noise of the gala fanfare and hearing his loved ones interacting with a façade of him gnaw deeply at him. His eyes return to the screen. Anger grills him as he watches his wife, his daughter, his family and friends enjoy a momentous occasion—their special night, their anniversary—with another man. He lies there, helpless, strapped to the bed, tormented by the sight of this inhuman imitation that has replaced him.

I hate Erica.

———— ∞ ————

AS THE IMPOSTER lifts his arm high to toast Jill, he moans, "Ohhhhhhh, my back." Pretending to be in pain, he grabs his lower back and rubs it. His deception fools Madi, who walks up between Jeremy and him.

"What's the matter Dad? Is your MLC kicking in?"

He wraps his arm around Madi's neck and teases her as the two of them walk off. "The world does not need to know I'm getting old."

Madi advises, "You should just dance with Mom. They say dancing soothes the pain."

The lookalike father chuckles. "And where did you learn that?"

"School."

"Incorrectly. So, now they're teaching incorrect quotes?"

"No, Dad, I just added my own spin to it. Oh, you're so apropo."

"Hmmm...apropo, another new word. I'm impressed."

The two chuckle and walk into the main hall joining Jeremy and the other guests.

Jill stands at the podium in the main hall, making her gracious speech. "To my friends, family, and critics, who I hope will give me a raving ten review..." Everyone chuckles. "A toast to all of you." She raises her champagne glass to the guests. "Thank you for supporting the Teresa Young Shelter for Battered Women and celebrating my most prized work. This has been a tremendous year."

Jill unveils a marquee that flashes "$10,000,000." Cheers echo throughout the hall. Applause rings out, champagne corks pop, and confetti streams down from the ceiling.

"Ten million dollars!" Jill continues. "Thank you!"

Mrs. Johnson walks up behind the double and sensuously sweeps her hand across the back of his shoulder. Expecting to play their usual harmless flirtation game, she gently squeezes his shoulder as if she was massaging a love. "Hello, handsome."

He ignores her and Mrs. Johnson repeats, "Hello, handsome. You're avoiding me?"

His eyes turn white and from his inside jacket pocket, he pulls out a pair of shades to conceal his eyes from Mrs. Johnson. "I am," he says abruptly.

Mrs. Johnson wasn't expecting that brush off but is teasingly persistent. "She's lovely, but I'm better looking."

He responds, "Are you? And here, I thought you were just basic. Mirror, mirror on the wall, who's the beauty of them all? Why, Mrs. Johnson, it ain't you, with those wrinkles and all."

"What? What did you say?"

"In fact, I think the mirror cracked." He smirks and takes a sip of champagne.

Surprised and offended by his comments, Mrs. Johnson storms off.

Now back across the room at the podium, Jill continues her speech. "To my husband and daughter—my darlings, the past twenty years have been a celebration every year and every day. I love you. Happy anniversary, sweetheart!"

A vase of beautifully arranged flowers sits nearby. Troy pulls a rosebud stem from the arrangement and sticks it into his fluted champagne glass, toasting Jill. He blows a kiss to her, and she catches it as she walks up to him. This façade of love and adoration is just that, but a great actor he is. He kisses her on the cheek then down the side of her face as if he could taste her inner love for him. His tongue swirl's ever so seductively in her ear.

"Oooh, a turn on. We're in public."

"I don't care." He whispers in her ear. "I could take you right here." Then, he wraps his arm around her waist, and pulls her body closer into his. She feels the hardness between his legs as it touches her from behind.

"Control that beast in you." She turns around and embraces him trying to subdue his unusually strong nature. "What happened to MLC?"

"It's on hiatus."

He kisses her again and she back to him. Everyone oohs and ahhs at them.

Madi blasts them from the microphone at the podium. "Ok, Mom and Dad, no Sex 101 classes here. So embarrassing."

The guest all laugh. Tango music begins to play from the intercom. As the music plays, the imposter gently releases his lips from Jill with a sweet peck and he spins her out, then pulls her back into his arms. She strokes his head sweeping her hand through his curly locks. Their eyes meet.

"Do you tango?" he asks.

She raises an eyebrow and seductively smiles. "Only with my lover."

He nibbles her ear and whispers, "Happy anniversary, darling."

As they tango to the music, Jill's curves sway to the rhythm of the music and his hands seductively trace every curve of her body. It's like his fingers are sculpting a beautiful work of art touching and following the lines of her curves.

<hr />

SLOW NAGGING DROPS of rain fall from the edge of the roof to the window sill outside Room 113. Troy pulls and tugs on the wrist and ankle restraints. Tears fill his eyes.

His heart felt like it had been ripped apart, being subjected to the scene of watching his wife being seduced by someone else and she returning that same seduction. He feels she should have known the difference. She should know he is an intruder of her heart and is not real. Helpless, he wails, "Ohhhhhhhhhhh, God, help me! Help me get out of here. Please, stop this madness!"

Erica pops out of the shadows and whispers in Troy's ear. "Now what day is this?"

Her sudden appearance startles him but angers him as well. His tears quickly dry up as he grimaces at the sight of her.

"What day is this? The day I resolve how much I detest, despise, and grossly hate you."

"Hate is a strong word that has no reason and can have horrible consequences. I wouldn't use that word so lightly," Erica warns. She attempts to kiss Troy, but he resists her advances and jerks his head away.

"You think you won't betray her love. She's betrayed everything that you cherish so dearly. Twenty years... How easy they have become void." Erica replays the scene over and over again of the tango dance when the lookalike spins Jill out and then back into his arms.

"Do you tango?" and "Only with my lover" resonate in Troy's ear.

Time passes. The clock on the wall shows 2:00 a.m., and the moonlight shines across Troy's bed. Erica's relentless torment showing Jill and the double's tango repeatedly flashes on and off the screen. Jill's words, "Only with my lover," ring constantly in his ear. He squeezes his fingers tight in a fist digging them so deep that the skin on his palm tears. Blood seeps through the cracks of his fingers. Troy pounds his fist on the bed, helpless.

He does not see Erica sitting in a dark corner with the remote, flashing the tango scene, on and off, on and off. What day is this?—hate, hate, hate.

Chapter 12

OH, WHAT A BEAUTIFUL DAY!

Nᴀɴᴄᴇ ᴇɴᴛᴇʀꜱ Tʀᴏʏ'ꜱ room, carrying a medication tray with the usual syringe, small bottle, and tablet sitting on it. She sets the medication tray next to Troy on the food table, but he does not stir. Once again, he didn't get much sleep from his late night and tortuous early morning. Signs of Erica's imposed sleeplessness begins to show on his face with the dark circles under his eyes.

Nance crosses over to the window and rips the curtains open. Her bubbly personality exudes cheerfulness. "Such a beautiful view." Troy awakens with squinted eyes as the sun rays hit them. Nance's voice is very vibrant. "Such a beautiful day."

Troy groggily opens his eyes wider. "Speak for yourself. I'm here. So what's beautiful about it?" He stares out the window consumed with feeling lost and abandoned.

Nance opens a window. "Fresh air. Breathe it all in." She inhales then exhales. "There's nothing like clean, fresh air after a hard rain." She gets a good look at him. "Wow!" Bad night, huh. Not much sleep." The dark circles underneath his eyes show how tired and weary he is. Troy rolls his eyes at her with much disdain. If only she would believe his story, perhaps this nightmare could end. She crosses over to Troy, straightens his blanket, and then eyes the traces of blood on the bed linen. "What's this?"

Troy opens the palms of his hands. Dried blood spots his palms.

"What were you trying to do?"

Troy cuts his eyes at Nance. "Die."

"Next time, hit an artery."

Troy curtly responds, "Leave a knife, then maybe I can."

Nance cuts Troy a sharp look. She pulls some alcohol swabs and bandages from the drawer next to his bed and begins to clean his palms and bandage the deep slits. Wanting to understand, she asks compassionately, "Along with your other ills, is this why you're in here?"

Troy fusses, "How many times must I tell you, I've been kidnapped!"

She doesn't yield to his accusations about Dr. Pendergrass and admonishes him. "Stop singing that song."

"How can I make you believe me? I don't belong in here. There's nothing wrong with me. She's crazy."

"She—who's the crazy one?" Nance grabs the syringe.

Fear races through Troy's mind as he watches Nance fill the syringe. The torment of the syringe angers him, but his rage is short-lived.

Troy pleads with her, "No, please don't. Don't, don't. I don't need it."

Nance stops. "This will help you."

"If you want to help me, then help me get out of here."

Nance puts the syringe down on the tray. "You know, all you patients have that in common. You don't belong in here. You want me to help you get out of here."

"I do. Look, I can make this worth your while if you help me."

"And how many times have I heard that tune? Let's see. There are twenty-five other patients here, and twenty-five times I've heard that. And now you make twenty-six." Nance gives him a brief smile. "Oh, and then I'll hear it again for the twenty-sixth thousandth time too—'cause I know each patient here has said it at least a hundred times—this is all a mistake."

"It is. My name is Troy Norton."

"No kidding," mocks Nance, "and you're not the President of the United States?"

Agitated and even more frustrated, Troy rips at the restraints, trying to break the bonds to his freedom. "Cut me loose, please. I'll make it worth it."

"What?"

"Cut me loose! I'll make it worth your while."

Nance eyes him. "Bribery. Gets better."

"One million right now and $250,000 every year for the rest of your life. Just help me escape."

"Unbelievable. I'm suppose to believe you—suicidal, hallucinating, and locked up in a mental institution. I'm suppose to believe that you can get that kind of money?"

"I'm a Senior VP at Georgia Federal. You've got to believe me, don't you?"

Nance hesitates as she thinks about all that has just transpired. "Diamonds may be a girl's best friend, but green gives me choices."

"Good."

Troy gives Nance his bank account code and tells her, "the money is yours for helping me." His mind wonders...*Does Nance believe me? Will she help me?*

Nance pulls her cell phone out. "Now give me the number."

Relieved and hopeful, Troy calls out, "Five, five, five, one, six, four, six, two, one, one. You got that?"

She enters the numbers in her cell phone. He asks Nance to repeat it back to him. She repeats, "Five, five, five, sixteen, forty-six, two, one, one."

"Now, when you get the money, you'll know I was telling the truth. Then please, please call my wife." Troy stretches his fingers to touch Nance's hand, hoping he has a friend now who will help him. "Please call her. Please hurry."

Nance, baffled and somewhat unsure of what to do or believe, smiles and hangs a fresh IV bag. She pities this man who she believes is mentally deranged. And the idea that the famous doctor and she conspired in his kidnapping is absurd. After all, why would he end up in Pendergrass Sanitarium, but for no other reason than a troubled unstable mind?

Troy pleads with Nance. "No more medication. The after effects are so horrific."

"Got to," she insists. "Doctors orders."

He wrestles with the IV. "No, no, no! Damn it, woman! She kidnapped me."

Troy, agitated and angry, twist and turns trying to prevent Nance from injecting the syringe into the IV tubing line but with no success. The solution flows down the tube toward his arm and Nance squeezes the bag to help the solution travel faster. The liquid enters his body. In seconds, his body jerks even harder than the other times.

Nance tries to comfort him. "Look, this is to help you."

Troy sluggish responds, "Don't help me anymore." He shivers. His eyes open, then roll back in his head. The tremors come on harder, and the shivering is more intense. She braces his shoulders to steady him as she looks down at her watch, timing his tremors. Troy shakes more and more, harder and harder. He breaks into a cold sweat, then almost instantly the tremors subside.

Nance pats Troy on the arm and comforts him. "Now, that wasn't so bad."

His voice is groggy and speech slurred. "Fuuuuuck…" Then his eyes close, asleep. Probably more needed than he realized. After days and nights of tortuous events and sleepless nights, Nance may have done him a favor.

Moments later at the nurses' station, Nance walks up to Erica, who reads a chart on a computerized tablet. She expresses her concern about Troy.

"His tremors were harder this time. Maybe the dosage should be reduced," she suggests.

"What?" Erica says, a bit miffed. "Well, aren't you the concerned one. So you're the doctor now?"

Nance responds defensively, "No, no, that's not what I meant. No harm meant."

Erica pacifies her. "No harm taken. I'll review the dosage. Thank you, Dr. Nance."

Nance, a little worried by the obvious, manages a smile and walks back down the hall. She pokes her head in Troy's room. "How you doing, sweet thang?"

Troy opens his eyes and flicks a middle finger at her. He sluggishly stumbles through the words, "Fuck...you."

"Got it—better. Uh-huh, and don't worry, I'll take care of that business for you."

Nance backs out of Troy's door and bumps into Erica, who's standing behind her.

Erica suspiciously asks, "What business?"

"Oh, Dr. Pendergrass, that's a real nutcase in there. He gave me this number. Said he was going to give me a million dollars right now and two hundred and fifty grand every year for the rest of my life."

"And you believe that?"

"Like I need a hole in my head." As the two women walk up to the nurses' station, Nance tears the paper into shreds and tosses it into the trash. "Yeah, right, a real nutcase, Dr. Pendergrass."

Erica chuckles and says to Nance. "It's good to know I can count on you." She pats Nance on her back, a gesture to show her appreciation for her loyalty as an employee.

Nance continues making her rounds. She pokes her head in and out of different patients' rooms, checking on them and administering meds. Later, Erica steps out of her office into the hallway and calls. "Nance, step in here for a second."

"Sure thing, Dr. Pendergrass. Just need to look in on one more."

Nance enters the next room, and hears the familiar repetitive words ring in her ear, "Am I going home now? Am I going home now?"

After making her rounds, Nance enters Dr. Pendergrass' dark office. Moonlight peeps through the curtains, shining on several shelves of psychology books on insects and psychology medicine. "This office gives me the creeps," she mutters.

Raindrops start falling outside. An aquarium with minicaves inside sits in a corner. At the caves' dark entrance, pink fluorescent eyes flicker, unnoticed by Nance.

She calls out, "Dr. Pendergrass?"

A black-gloved hand quickly comes from behind her and plunges the contents of a syringe into the side of Nance's neck. She collapses to the floor.

***

HOURS LATER, RAIN drops pour down the windowpane, hitting it harder and harder. Nance barely comes out of an unconscious state to a view of video frames—Troy, Jill, and Madi in different scenes, together and individually. Edited snapshots taken of him at the recreation center, the bank and parking garage, playing basketball with Madi, and different shots of Troy and Jill, wrapped in each other's arms making love, project from the video frames. The projection on the wall flashes on and off. Nance sits in a leather winged-back chair, and her eyes groggily open, then shut again. Duct tape covers her mouth, and a rope, crisscrossed around her chest to her feet, hugs her body tightly. Her hands are bound behind her back.

Erica leans into her ear. "Wake up, Miss Sweet Thang. Doctor Nance, wake up now. I need you to focus."

Nance does not stir because she is still somewhat unconscious. Erica taps Nance's face several times and grabs her chin, shaking it. She slowly comes to, blurry-eyed, focusing on the video pictures of Troy, Jill, and

Madi. She does not understand what is going on. Her eyes dart back and forth as she follows the flashing video. She moans like a whimpering dog.

Erica walks into her view. She relishes the thought that perhaps an adversary has been captured in her snare. In Erica's twisted mind, Nance was someone perceived as a threat.

"Silly girl."

Nance whimpers even more, pleading for Erica to free her. "Uh uhnnnn," she cries out.

Erica snatches the tape off her mouth. "What did you say?"

"Ouch!" Nance flinches. "What? Why?"

"You thought you could take him from me."

"What are you talking about?"

"I've waited twenty years, and neither you nor his wife are going to take him from me."

"Take who?"

Erica spills out, "I'm not a fool. I know what you're trying to do."

Revelation time. It all makes sense to Nance now, maybe a little too late. "Troy? Troy, he—he wasn't lying. You are—"

"—crazy," Erica finishes Nance's sentence. "If loving a man as much as I love him is crazy, then I'm crazy in love."

Erica crosses over to the aquarium where two pair of padded forceps hang over the side. Pink fluorescent eyes flicker from the dark entrance of the minicaves lined across the aquarium gravel floor.

Erica grabs several pincers, dragging white scorpions out from the caves with each forcep. Their barbed tails curl, repeatedly striking the forceps. Milky white secretions drip down the forceps.

"No! No!" Nance shrieks as Erica comes closer to her dangling the white scorpions.

"It'll only hurt a little."

Tears stream down Nance's face. She's screams out in fear. "Help! Somebody help me!" But her outcry goes unnoticed.

Erica laughs. "Silly, silly girl. Remember the acoustics work I had done? No one can hear you. No one."

Nance panics. "The nurses' station—they can see you."

"Are you a patient here? Look around. See any cameras in here?"

Nance's eyes dart back and forth from corner to corner and sees an empty room filled with only a video frame of pictures, a desk and couch, bookshelves filled with books and two chairs.

"Please, no! Dr, Pendergrass, I'm begging you. I'm begging. I promise I won't tell anyone."

Erica crosses over to the bookshelf. "Tell you what. You know, I'm a student of war." She pulls a book from her shelf. "Have you ever read *The Art of War* by Sun Tzu? Probably not. Too much for that small brain of yours."

Nance gestures no, shaking her head back and forth.

"You're so busy trying to take away another woman's man. Well, if you're going to play that game, then you should learn the art of war. Sun Tzu says, "Victorious warriors win first and then go to war.""

Erica drops the scorpions on Nance from each forceps.

Nance screams out in pain as each one repeatedly stings her. She squirms and flinches with each sting, screaming out loud, loud, and louder.

In the hallway there is dead silence from the night. The RNs making their rounds in the hallway make no attempt to respond to Nance's screams; after all, her screams are silent to them. At the nurses' station, Nurse Penny and Robby laugh and talk, oblivious to her outcry because there is no camera to allow viewing inside of Erica's office.

Erica leans in and brags, "I'm a victorious warrior and I'm helping you keep your promise."

Nance's head drops to her chest. Her cold eyes stare out. Drool slides down the side of her chin.

NEXT MORNING, IT'S shift change at the nurses' station. Nance would have relieved her at 6:00am so Nurse Penny fusses about her being late to Robby. She looks at the clock on her computer monitor, which shows 7:30 a.m.

Robby sarcastically remarks, "Oh, what a beautiful day."

Nurse Penny is perturbed. "Yeah, right. My day off, and Nance's running late. Beautiful."

Chapter 13

I Am My Wife's Keeper

THUNDER ROARS ON the stormy morning. A rain waterfall streams down the windowpane outside Troy's room. Erica enters, cheerful, carrying a food tray along with the usual syringe and IV bag.

"Good morning, love. Breakfast. I dreamed of serving you breakfast in bed, and then we'd make love."

The thought of that intimacy disgusts Troy. He rolls his eyes at her and says dismally, "It's raining."

"Yes it is," she says enthusiastically.

"And you are my waking nightmare. I'm sad. Where's Nance?" Troy sighs.

She ignores his negative comments and sits the food tray next to Troy's bed. "Don't you want my passion, too?"

"Give me a gun. I'd rather take a bullet in the head."

Erica chuckles. "You're such a kidder."

Troy glances at Erica, wondering, *Does she hear herself?* Has she heard anything he's said? Is she really that manic that she can't tell reality from make-believe?

"I want one thing, and that is for this nightmare to end right now." Again he asks, "Where's Nance?"

Erica says, "Nightmare? It's only begun. And Nance, she didn't come in today." She flips the screen on.

⁂

JILL STANDS AT the window looking out and is distracted by the constant explosive barking of Ron's dog, Fifi. She pulls the curtains back to get a better look while the double pretends he is engaged with one of his midlife crisis therapy channels on cooking in their island kitchen. With his back turned away from Jill, he watches the screen, mimicking the expert chef, chopping onions on the block in the middle of the kitchen with the perfection of a real chef island kitchen, which is not an arduous act for him. Afterall, he is a robot.

"Isn't Ron gone?" she asks.

"Yeah." He tries to avoid the subject and continues, "This is going to be good."

"What?"

"My salad."

"Salad?" She wonders why Fifi is at home all alone when Ron normally takes her with him on trips or to the dog kennel. "Aren't you even bothered by the fact that Ron's gone, and Fifi is home alone? That's just not like him to leave Fifi like that."

The imposter is annoyed with her questioning. "I'm not my brother's keeper."

"He's your best friend. Something could be wrong."

He retorts, "Are you deliberately trying to make this an argument?"

"Of course not. I'm just concerned, and I would think you'd be, too, about your best friend of over twenty years."

"Look, I don't know where Ron is. He's probably gone fishing, and unlike me, he is a widower, a free man. He doesn't have to answer to anyone."

"Meaning?" Jill asks.

He quickly dismisses the subject ignoring her and continues chopping the onions.

"You know, I'm really growing tired of your behavior. You need to see a doctor, the mental kind. Maybe I'll go check on Fifi." Agitated, Jill grabs a dish towel, dries her hands, and throws it down hard on the counter. An unhappy cat, she ferrets through a drawer of whatnots and survey papers.

"There's nothing in this drawer, but your surveys. I...I can't find it."

"Find what?"

"The key to Ron's house."

He tells Jill that he will take care of the dog, but her pesky distraction does not deter him from his MLC therapy session cooking. As Fifi's nagging bark riles him more, he chops the onions even harder and faster.

Jill wants him to go and tend to Fifi, now. She is deliberate in her hunt as she continues to rummage through the drawer.

Fifi barks.

Jill fusses, "All I ask is for you to go now!"

Jill's nagging and Fifi's annoying bark irritate him. His eyes turn white. He retorts, "I'll take care of the dog, Jill. Don't worry about it."

Fifi barks mightily several times.

"Honey, now, please!" Jill demands.

Annoyed, he chops the onions even faster, trying to ignore Jill and Fifi, both ringing in his ears like the grinding wheels of a rail train on the tracks trying to break. His acute computer abilities turn the television volume up, louder, louder, and louder, trying to drown out her voice as well as Fifi's. Suddenly, his white eyes change to clear.

While Troy frantically watches this turmoil, he pulls and tugs at the straps pinning him to the bed. He screams at Erica. "His eyes, what's happening? His eyes! Erica!"

Madi walks in and grabs an apple from a fruit basket sitting on the counter. "Dad, are you getting hard of hearing too?" She moves the television remote over to the counter closer to him so he can turn the volume down. "Volume, Dad. Turn it down!" she yells back as she exits. "Rosie and I are doing our thing. Later." The front door shuts.

The lookalike's computerized telepathic ability presses the volume button, lowering the sound.

Jill shakes her head, perplexed. How could the volume decrease when it appeared that the remote was not in her husband's hand? In her mind, that's inconceivable—no one could do that. She second-guesses herself and tosses it off, believing that she must be seeing things.

Troy cries out, watching, "It's not me, Jill. Can't you see? Trust your gut, it's not me!" He wrestles with the wrist and ankle straps, squirming and twisting.

Fifi's distracting bark gets Jill's attention again. She pulls the curtains back, looking out the window, grumbling at the imposter. "Take care of the dog."

"Sure."

In the next second, the chopping knife sails past the side of her face, raising the fine hairs on her skin, barely missing her cheek. Jill screams from fear and intimidation.

"What's wrong with you?"

The knife pins the curtain back to the wall. Helpless, defenseless, and not able to protect the woman he loves, Troy yells at the screen. "I'll kill you! I'll kill you!" His wrist and ankles, black and blue, bear the scars of the many times he's tried to break loose.

The lookalike brushes up against Jill's cheek with his. His eyes are white, but she doesn't see them. He slides the knife from the curtain. She's more than angry and scolds him.

"What is going on with you? First your MLC. Now you're trying to kill me. You're totally out of control."

Troy yells out. "His eyes. Look at his eyes, Jill." But his words cannot be heard by Jill. Afterall, it is a screen that he speaks to.

The double grabs Jill from behind and wraps his arms around her, pleading with her to forgive him. "I'm sorry. I don't know what got into me."

She shoves her husband away and storms off, never noticing his eyes. She runs up the stairs to the bedroom and slams the door.

Troy, fearing for her life, screams, "Lock the door! Lock the door!"

The double climbs up the stairs. His eyes, repulsively white. "Jill! Darling! I'm sorry. I'm coming for you." He steps closer and closer to the bedroom door.

In a rage, Troy asks Erica, "His eyes—what's wrong with his eyes?"

"He has the eyes of a killer." Erica emphatically responds.

"Lock the door, Jill! He's not me—lock the door!"

As he approaches the door, the door knob clicks from Jill locking it. He rattles the doorknob and turns it to find it locked. "Honey, unlock the door." He jiggles the doorknob again. "Jill, open the door."

"No! This MLC—you're changing."

"I'm sorry. I didn't mean to frighten you. I would never hurt you. C'mon, open the door. Babe, I love you."

Jill reaches for the doorknob to unlock it.

Troy cries out, pounding the bed with his fist. "No, Jill, no!"

Fifi barks ferociously like a guard dog. Jill stops. "Go! Check the dog, Troy, my darling husband," with a bit of sarcasm in her voice. She crosses over to the bathroom and slams the door.

Troy is outraged but relieved that for now it appears she is safe. His eyes water and he feels the pain of knowing that he could do nothing to help her. Hearing his wife call his enemy by his name and refer to him as husband gnaws at his heart. He screams.

"Erica!"

Chapter 14

BETRAYAL

"THIS IS WHAT happens when you're a bad boy."

Troy is puzzled at Erica's remarks and shouts at her. "Bad boy! Your creation just tried to kill my wife."

Erica belligerently responds, "That is the point. I should be angry with you. Huh, you and that silly nurse… Flirting with her."

Troy barks back, "I was not."

"Really!" she blurts out. Then Erica cries, "And now your wife. I want you to love me. I want you to love me!" She's upset and runs out of the room.

Troy pulls at the restraints. He notices that the threads have unraveled a little at the ends, but escape still seems so distant.

Erica comes back carrying a small grey trash can. Troy stops pulling so as not to arouse any suspicion to the unraveled threads.

She crosses over to Troy and empties the trash can contents all over his chest and stomach. He squirms, trying to avoid the spillage of partially empty coffee cups, wads of used tissue paper, pencil shavings, torn paper, and other trash. Although loosened some, the tight reins of the restraints still restrict his movement.

She muddles through the torn pieces of paper with the plastic-capped syringe tip. "How much was it?"

Surprised that she knows, Troy cuts his eyes at her and asks, "What are you talking about?"

Erica pops the plastic cap off the syringe needle and begins to spread the torn pieces of paper around pricking him as she sweeps through the trash across his chest and stomach. She slides several pieces of papers together. "Now what was the plan?"

It starts raining. Small traces of blood seep through the paper as she slides a torn piece with a dollar sign and the number two written on it across his chest. He moans from the pricking. The raindrops pound harder, each echoing like the hoofs of a horse trampling its victim in a dark tunnel. Erica pricks his skin more as she slides the numbers together like a scrabble game maze when one tries to find the right letters to form a word. Another number—she stabs through the paper with the needle.

"Uhnn," he groans.

She calls out, "The number five. And the winner is… zero." Erica pricks his skin again dragging over the number zero with a comma next to the numbers two and five. Her cold eyes penetrate Troy's. The raindrops pound the windowpane harder, harder, and harder.

"$250,000? Slut! This was your plan."

Troy repudiates her accusations. "What plan? I don't know what you're talking about."

But Erica does not believe him and abhors his innocent behavior. She does not accept his actions and repeatedly sticks him with the needle as she becomes more and more agitated with him.

"Do you take me for a fool?"

He cringes and moans with each relentless stick. More blood seeps through the paper. Erica pricks Troy several times on the stomach. With each painful jab, he squints, frowns, and moans even more. "Erica!" He screams out.

She pricks him again, dragging the torn pieces of paper together to form the numbers on an imaginary straight line, just like her imagined love obsession.

"Erica! Stop! I'm not a pin cushion."

"What? What did you say?"

"Not a pin cushion. Stop!" He moans.

She catches herself when she sees the thin line of blood slowly running down his side.

"You want to leave me, don't you?" She grips the syringe tightly in her hands.

Troy watches her every move, careful not to say the wrong words inciting her venomous anger even more. For if he does, he knows he might receive more than just a prick—more like a needle plunged deep inside of him. He screams, "What are you doing?"

Thunder roars.

Troy squirms and breathes hard. "No! Erica, no!"

But even with his unspoken words, her rage is uncontrollable. She raises the syringe high about to stab the needle deep inside him. Her tears of pain drop on Troy and mixes with his blood. She cries, "You wanted her over me."

She stabs the pillow several times, missing his face only by a hair because Troy quickly turned his head away. She yells, "You wanted her over me! Never! Never! Never! I'm never gonna let you go."

A moment later, Erica, now eerily calm, says, "The rain has stopped. I'm sorry I lost control."

Sweat beads roll down Troy's face.

Erica calmly continues, "Rain makes me sad, and sometimes I get so angry that control becomes history. Besides, it doesn't matter. I put an end to that."

Panic riddles Troy's face. "What did you do?"

"Kiss me," she demands.

"What did you do?" Troy demands.

Erica kisses Troy roughly. He twists and turns his head away to avoid her touch. Her lips press painfully against his. Troy spits in her face, which angers her. She wipes her face and licks her finger.

"Love is sweet and I'm the better woman for you."

With intense emotion and force, she grabs his chin with one hand and penetrates his stare with her piercing eyes while the fingers of her other hand sensuously travel down his chest.

"Stop, Erica. Tell me. What did you do?"

She moves downward and gently massages between his legs.

"No, no, no, no, no, no." He violently twists to keep from succumbing to her touch.

"You want me. I know you do."

"No, no. Stop! I love Jill. I'll never betray her love."

Erica presses the remote sitting on the nightstand. The TV screen pops on. Erica says, "But she's betrayed you. She's betrayed your love. Just like I want you, she wants him."

Jill and the lookalike make love. She flips him over. Her hand travels down his chest to his inner thighs. Jill whispers in his ear, "I want you." Her tongue seductively circles his ear.

Helpless turmoil and anger consume him as he watches his wife make love to another man, to a man who is her killer. "This is your deceit, not hers." Troy squirms, rocking his head back and forth. "No! Stop. Stop, Erica, stop! Turn it off! Off! You can't force me to love you."

"Really, now."

"No, you'll never have my love."

Erica begins stripping her clothes off. She takes her lab coat off and tosses it; over a chair in the corner. Then, she seductively unbuttons her top and hikes her pencil skirt up as she climbs on top of him.

"I don't want you. Stop this. I'm begging you. For the love of God, stop this insanity."

Erica ignores his plea. Instead, she torments him more, turning the volume up on the screen.

Ohhhhh! Jill moans with pleasure as he pumps her from behind. He penetrates her deeply with each riding thrust. She grips the bed comforter squeezing bunches of single rose petals between her fingers that cover the bed linen. The bedroom lighting is sensuously subdued. Only the dim flicker of light from the candles around the room and the radiant moonlight gives enough brightness to show Jill pushing feverishly back in to him. Troy's favorite song of an unending love plays in the background. She moans with pleasure. "Oh-oh-oh-oh-ohhhhh."

Forced to watch his wife in this act that one would normally perceive as betrayal, his eyes water. But the reality of knowing that Erica has caused this and Jill is not responsible grinds at him. His hatred toward Erica grows even more.

In the midst of Jill's intimate moment the lookalike ask, "Am I forgiven?"

"Only if you promise to give me a repeat performance. Making up with you is pure pleasurable raw sex. Just the way I love it with you." Jill collapses back on the bed.

Meanwhile his virtual internal monitor flashes back to when he entered Ron's house. Fifi was barking incessantly at him. She recognized him as a friend not foe wagging her tail. She calmly stopped barking. He fondly pets her. But just as quickly as he began to pet Fifi, she snapped at his hand, tearing into his synthetic skin. Fifi growled and snarled at him. Her canine senses detected the coldness of an inanimate object, a nonhuman.

His eyes turned white.

Snap! The growling and snarling stop. Dead silence. The imposter posing as Troy stood over Fifi's lifeless body, her stiff head contorted from a broken neck. As he walks back home, he picks a bunch of peach stemmed roses from the yard and doesn't flinch from the thorns that stick him before his intimate moment with Jill. He stops at the kitchen counter and pulls a pair of wire cutters out from a drawer. He snips the thorns and cuts the petals for their romantic interlude.

Now later with Jill after their lovemaking, he continues his apology. "I didn't mean to scare you. I don't know what got into me. I'm so sorry. Forgive me?"

"Ok, you're forgiven this time, Mr. MLC." Jill kisses him deeply.

Tears roll down Troy's face as he listens to the sounds of their lovemaking, of Jill's moaning. "Oh, oh, oh, oh, ohhhhhhhhhh."

Erica turns the screen off. She straddles Troy and kisses all over his face. Her lips meet his, and then she tries to invade his mouth with her tongue, but he presses his lips tightly together to stop this violation, this unwanted intrusion.

"No, no, no, Erica. Stop!" Twisting, squirming, and pulling at the restraints, he avoids her caresses, flinging his head from side to side.

Erica's tongue proceeds south between his legs. "I know you want me, and I want to feel you inside of me." Excited and anxious, Erica struggles to take her panties off.

He gives up and lies there like a weak, dehumanized, castrated man totally surrendering to her power and control. He is a prisoner without the possibility of saving his love or himself.

Then a sudden change.

"Let me help you," Troy offers.

Surprised by his sudden change in temperament, Erica says, "What? Don't toy with me."

"Take these off, and I can show you how I really feel."

Erica slides down from on top of Troy. "I don't believe you."

Troy concedes. "No, you were right. It should have been you all along. Hurry, let me show you how I really feel."

Erica, desperate for his love, circles Troy's face with kisses and anxiously rushes over to her lab coat. She pulls a key from her pocket and unlocks the metal locking mechanism on the wrist restraint.

Reluctantly, Troy rubs Erica's back.

She starts to unlock the ankle restraint but hesitates. "You are being truthful?"

"Trust me, I can't keep this up all day," he says, looking down at the stiffness between his legs. "Hurry, so we can—"

"—make love." Quickly, Erica unlocks an ankle restraint. She starts to unlock the other but stops. "I trust you, but I'm not stupid. One ankle, one wrist."

Cunning, Troy asks, "How can I give all of me if I'm strapped down?"

"Betrayal."

Troy kisses Erica passionately. His eyes water.

Erica drops her skirt and climbs on top of Troy. She kisses his lips and moves downward, but her efforts to seduce him are uninteresting, unwanted, and resented.

Then, the sanitarium emergency alert rings in her ear through a Bluetooth earplug. Erica clutches her ear. "Damn. No, no, no! Not now."

"What?" Troy asks.

Erica presses the earpiece deeper into her ear, trying to hear better. "This better be good. Talk to me."

Troy, excitedly curious, asks again, "What's going on?"

Furious, Erica says, "Joe!" Annoyed, she takes a deep breath. "Give him something." She waits to hear if the heated moment of pleasure with Troy can continue. "Say it again? Yeah, right. Psycho."

Erica puts her skirt back on but leaves the lab coat lying on the chair. She composes herself tucking the blouse inside the skirt.

"Erica, what's wrong?"

She stands at the door and hesitates, sensing sincerity in his voice. "You really want me."

He fakes a smile.

She crosses back over to Troy and kisses him, then quickly exits.

Troy wipes his lips feverishly, trying to remove any trace of Erica's touch on his lips. Then, finding a way to escape. He anxiously hops up off the bed and struggles stretching toward the lab coat, with no success.

"Damn."

Chapter 15

THE GREAT ESCAPE

ERICA BURSTS THROUGH the door. Two CNAs corner Joe, who is dressed in a pair of checkered pajamas—pants and top. Every time the CNAs get closer to Joe, he swings his arms at them wildly, so they back off. This time, Joe's shuffling is more determined and unrelenting. It resembles more of a march back and forth as he repeats, "It's time to go home now. It's time to go home now."

Erica is livid and snaps at Joe. "Ok, Joe, I don't have time for this." For she anxiously wants to return to Troy and pickup where she left off.

Joe charges through the CNAs toward the door.

Back in Room 113, Troy works on escaping. He dumps the food and IV bag sitting on the tray onto the floor. He stretches toward the chair and uses the tray to hook the arm of the chair. Troy barely touches the top edge of the chair, when the grip of the wrist and ankle restraints snap Troy back hard to the floor. The restraints are not flimsy and he did not expect what would happen next. The stretching caused a digital counter to engage a feature where a metal locking mechanism tightens around the wrist. As Troy has stretched and pulled on the reins attached to the metal locks and once loosened to 80 percent, the nanosensors send a digital reading to the locking mechanism. The lock automatically tightens and the teeth of the metal lock painfully clamp tighter around Troy's wrist, almost cutting his circulation off. "Ahhhhhh, what's happening?" He screams out in excruciating pain. The pain is so horrific, he falls to his knees.

Meanwhile, it appears Joe might be getting the best of the CNAs in his room. He violently swings at them, trying to stave them off.

Erica orders the CNAs, "Get him. Get him!"

"Time to go home now. Time to go home now. Time to go—"

The two CNAs rush Joe and wrestle him down to the floor.

Erica gets in Joe's face. "And, where the fuck do you think you're going?"

⊱⊰

Physically and mentally exhausted from the pain of the metal lock, Troy falls back on the bed. Now at zero percent, the tight grip of the locking mechanism has released around his wrist and it seems hope for escape is dismal. He did not anticipate this hurdle. What can he do? His eyes focus on the IV tubing and travel down to the needle—an opportunity. He squints in pain as he pulls the needle from the vein in his arm with his free hand. Then he bends the needle to make a hook and unwinds the IV cord to give it more length; he aims the needle at the chair, throwing the cord several times at the lab coat but missing each time.

"Damn, damn, damn."

Back in the room with Joe, the CNAs hold him down to the floor. Erica climbs on top of him.

Joe looks at her as if he is pleading to a kinder side. But kindness is absent to her emotional repertoire. Quickly, he returns to his catatonic state. "Home. I wanna go home now."

She plunges the needle into his arm. Immediately, his body relaxes and curls up into a fetal position, asleep. Erica confidently says, "Yeah, right. You can go home now."

TROY TRIES AGAIN and steps too far out of range; the clamps quickly begin to tighten, tearing into his skin. He cries out as blood starts to seep from under his skin. Too much farther might burst a vessel in his wrist. He steps back into the safety zone closer to the bed and the clamping stops.

One final try—Troy aims the needle at the lab coat, hoping for success this time. He throws it again. This time, the needle stabs the coat, hooking into it. He clenches his fist tight. "Yes!" A gesture, that perhaps escape is not so far away. Troy carefully pulls the coat toward him, mindful of the range he should stay within to keep the metal wristband from clamping, but the lab coat falls to the floor. "Aw, no, no, no, no, no."

However, the needle stays embedded. He reels the coat in closer to him. "I can do it. I can do this." He breathes hard. Sweat bubbles perforate his face. "Come on, baby, come on." When he has the lab coat within reach, he snatches it from the floor. "God, I love you."

He unlocks the metal locking mechanism, but before he sees freedom, Erica bursts through the door, a bit miffed.

"And where do you think you're going? Especially when you said you wanted me."

Troy, repulsed by the idea, retorts, "Over my dead body."

Erica snarls. "Don't push me." She talks through the Bluetooth earplug. "I need you in here, now!"

She's furious. "You think you're smart. You think you're gonna, what, get away…make your great escape? Huh, to save them. I control you." Erica pulls out the big screen remote. "It will give me great pleasure to watch your precious Jill be blown away. With just the touch of the remote, she will be gone forever." Erica refers to the same remote that she has used to torture Troy with.

Troy dives at Erica and wraps his hands around her neck, choking her. She gasps for air.

He yells at her. "I hate you. Die. Die."

The two CNAs rush in and tackle him, wrestling Troy down. They pry his hands finger by finger from his tight grip around her neck.

He screams, "I hate you, Erica. I hate you!"

Erica collects herself. "Hold him down."

The CNAs try to corner him but Troy belts one of them several times, and he drops to the floor. At the same time, the other CNA grabs him from behind and Troy head butts him hard in the face bloodying his nose. The CNA grabs his nose that bleeds profusely. Another CNA rushes into the room and Troy applies some of the karate fighting tactics that he learned as a counter-operative. He kicks his foot into the CNA's chest sending him sailing down to the floor. Then a fourth CNA charges into the room who is bigger than Troy. He slams into Troy causing him to stumble and giving way to the other three tackling him down. Erica rushes over and stabs the syringe in Troy's arm.

Troy trembles and falls to his knees, shivering and jerking. His face twitches and eyes roll back in his head, then close asleep.

———— ∞∞∞ ————

NIGHTTIME SHADOWS THE room. Troy's eyes groggily open as he hears the downpour thrashing against the window-pane. As he wakes, he has a fleeting moment of hope thinking that he had escaped. Then he moves and feels the weight of the restraints tugging at both his wrists and ankles again. Helplessness and doom consume him. He yells at the top of his lungs, "Oh, God!"

Erica steps out of the shadows, startling him. Fear races through his mind.

Furious, Erica lashes at him with her angry tongue. "You're a liar. You're a cruel small man that takes my love for granted. I really thought you wanted me."

Troy angrily responds, "You're the liar. You have a sick twisted mind and somehow you have convinced yourself of a lie that something existed between us."

"No-no-no-no, Stop! I won't listen." She cups her hands around her ears trying to block out what he is say-ing, but he continues.

"There's nothing, nothing between us. Never has been and never will. I could never love you."

Erica becomes hysterical and lambasts him as she paces back and forth. "Stop! Stop! I want listen to your lies. I know you don't mean any of this."

In an instant, her demeanor changes. She calms down and responds as if Troy had not said a word and his discontentment of her was completely erased from her mind. "I know you did not mean any of this. It was just a misunderstanding and couples in love have that sometime."

"You're sick. Have you not heard anything I've said? Let me repeat it. There is no you and me. Couples, I'd rather be dead."

"Dead, no. Persuaded, yes." Erica crosses over to the aquarium. "You know persuasion can be difficult, and it establishes rapport. And I don't think I've established a rapport with you."

Troy's eyes follow her as she taps the side of the aquarium. He watches her relentlessly unsure of what torture will happen next. But for certain, he is sure it will not be pleasant.

She continues explaining. "And there are three parts to persuading someone: Rapport, which we've clearly established that we don't have. Authority—"

Troy interjects, "You have that over me." He pulls and tugs at the wrist and ankle restraints.

Erica smirks. "Huh, and finally, a backup plan for nonbelievers. You're a nonbeliever. But, I'll shoot for two out of three, authority and the backup plan. So how do I persuade you to be a believer?" Her words are disturbing, and the hard rain pounding against the windows intimidates him even more with an uneasy feeling.

A pair of long sponge-tip forceps hangs over the aquarium side. She seductively strokes them as if she were making love to Troy. "We always relate the color white to cleanliness, goodness, and purity, but it can be very painful." She grabs the forceps and taps the top of a minicave. Nothing happens. She taps several more times. "Come out. Come out." A coarse scratchy movement comes from inside the cave, then stops. Erica taps again.

Troy asks, "What's in there?"

Erica answers, "You know, white signifies death in some cultures."

Glowing pink eyes blink at the opening of the dark cave. Troy asks, "You're gonna kill me now? Please, do me the favor."

Erica taps the aquarium once more. Two-inch-long translucent pincers peek out from the dark caves. Erica grabs the pincers and drags an angry white albino scorpion out. The scorpion wrestles with the forceps, curling its elevated barbed tail readying itself for attack. It strikes them several times. Milky white secretion dribbles down the forceps. Erica carefully moves toward Troy with the scorpion dangling from the forceps.

She explains that her father was an entomologist who loved insects more than he loved her. She puts the scorpion down on the table next to Troy's bed. "My father worked for the National Intelligence and Security Agency (NISA) designing and creating spy toys."

The scorpion runs from side to side as Erica teases it blocking its path with the forceps. Her teasing angers the scorpion who stabs at the forceps several times.

"Insectobots—that's what he created."

The scorpion angrily spears at the forceps.

Erica explains that she never received her father's love, so she found love in another kind of family. She chuckles. "Which, by the way, became very useful."

Not understanding her, Troy frowns with a questioned look at Erica. She toys with the white albino scorpion, playing Russian roulette with her finger. Troy suspects Erica may have used the insects to kill, so he suggests, "Useful for whom, Nance?"

"Let's just say, she got a sting of an ending."

Erica dangles the scorpion over Troy.

Fear grips him as he flinches and clutches the blanket between his fingers. "Erica, no!"

The scorpion squirms and wriggles relentlessly, working itself from the forceps and falling on the blanket at Troy's feet. Again he flinches.

"Don't move," Erica instructs him.

Troy, fearful that the scorpion might attack him with its stinging barbed tail lies still, but fear overcomes him. He trembles.

Erica loves playing mind games. She is a master at taunting and teasing. "You know, a scorpion's sting can be very painful, paralyzing, mostly deadly."

The scorpion travels upward on the blanket toward his upper thigh. Erica torments him by outlining the detailed effects of a scorpion's sting.

"First, there's numbness."

The scorpion crawls up more around Troy's stomach. He panics. "No, no!"

"Then, your neurosensors are paralyzed. Your brain talks to your body, but it won't listen, because it can't."

The albino scorpion crawls up to his bare chest.

"Sweat beads will cover your face."

Troy's sorrowful eyes plead with Erica to stop her madness. He tries to appeal to whatever sanity remains in this insane woman, his psychotic nemesis.

She remarks, "Then there are the convulsions and difficulty breathing."

"I'm begging you Erica, please stop this. Get it off me." She ignores him and does not yield.

"He doesn't like it when you move."

The scorpion crawls toward his neck. Troy breathes hard. The breeze from his nostrils fans the scorpion's shell. It stops and eyeballs him with its beady pink eyes.

"Don't move." She cautions.

Troy holds his breath. The scorpion travels closer to his neck. His white skin begins to turn blue from lack of oxygen. Running out of air, he pants. The subtle breeze of his breathing brushes across the scorpion's hard white shell. The scorpion's heart gyrates wildly as it crawls around Troy's chest watching its prey with its pink beady eyes like any predator would.

STRIKE—the scorpion stabs Troy's chest several times.

He screams out, "Get it off me! Get it off!" Troy squirms, trying to knock the scorpion off, and flinches from the painful sting.

"Changed your mind?"

"Damn you! Do I have a choice?"

As Erica lifts the scorpion off of him with the forceps, she reminds him," we all have choices, but sometimes physical persuasion carries more weight in guiding those choices." A bit mordant, she teases, "Feeling a little light-headed?"

The room spins. Troy's head feels like a merry-go-round. "The antidote. Give it to me!"

Erica slowly crosses back over to the aquarium and drops the scorpion back inside. She teases the scorpion with the forceps. "Sweat bubbles should be popping up about right now."

Beads of sweat bathe his forehead, face, and neck. "Shaking yet?" Erica asks.

Goosebumps cover Troy's arms. He trembles as his eyes roll back in his head. "Erica, stop-p-p-p-p this madness. The antidote! Giv-v-v-v-ve it to me!"

"Oh, stop your whining. You're not dying. It's harmless. He doesn't have enough venom in him to do you any harm. But this one, well…it's hungry." She drags the large white pincers of a huge albino scorpion from the cave onto the aquarium gravel floor. "It wants you like I want you to love me." The scorpion fights, violently spearing the forceps several times. "I really love you, and I would go to any lengths to make you love me."

Erica turns the HDTV on. Finally, she is about to reveal her true intentions for Troy's family.

Jill lies in the lookalike's arms, asleep like a babe protected. But is she safe?

"Look at those beautiful eyes," Erica says. The double's eyes have changed to white. "I need to erase a few things so your judgment's not clouded," she scolds.

Troy vehemently responds, "You're the only thing clouding my mind."

She smiles with a certain kind of smirk. "Eyes tell a story. They tell what's hidden behind the real truth. And they can play tricks and be very deadly."

The imposter's eyes change to clear, revealing red, green, and yellow lead wires attached to an internal digital time bomb inside his head.

"A bomb!" Troy yells. "You want me, not them." He furiously wrestles with the restraints. Erica taunts Troy even more and whispers in his ear that Jill won't matter anymore, because she will be erased. Enraged, Troy pounds the bed with his fist. "I'll kill you. I'll kill you!"

The swinging balls on the wall clock tap each time the clock hands move. The clock shows midnight. Erica reminds Troy of the twenty years she's waited, after watching the one thing that she loved be taken away from her. But that is about to change.

"She has twenty hours to live."

The clock hand moves when the balls touch. Troy cries out, "For the love of Christ, don't. Don't do this. Please, I'm begging you."

Chapter 16

TIME PASSES

MINUTES AND HOURS pass. The early morning darkness shadows the room as the swinging balls' TAP TAP TAPPING rings in Troy's ears. The clock hand moves to 3:00 a.m. Troy wails, "Oh, God, help me help them. I promised."

His eyes, tired from lack of sleep and the torturous experience Erica has put him through, close sporadically. Every time he awakens, he frantically searches the room for something to stop Erica's madness, something to free him. Now his wrist and ankles are even more darker with black-and-blue stripes where he has continually yanked and pulled at the restraints. The blood spots on his wrists are dark red, almost maroon colored, from where the metal restraints clamped down so very tight and broke his skin.

Time passes. It's *8:30 a.m.*

12:30 p.m. Strange, no Erica. Where is she and what is she doing?

The clock ticks as the swinging balls TAP TAP TAP. Fourteen and a half hours have gone by. It's *5:30p.m* and still no Erica. Troy rambles in his thoughts going back and forth, escape, *there is none. I must find a way to escape. Where is she and what is she plotting next?* Finally, Erica enters, carrying a food tray and another intravenous bag. Troy follows her every move. Erica methodically hangs the bag on the IV stand next to the bed. First, she squeezes it to help the flow travel faster. Then she checks the line to make sure it is not twisted, unlike her twisted mind, spinning a web of pain.

"I'll do whatever you want. Just stop this. Don't hurt my family."

"Well, good afternoon to me." Erica sits down next to him on the bed. She slices the meat on the plate, meticulously cutting it into equal-size pieces like a well-thought-out process. But the fact that he shows no interest in her is frustrating. Her impatience and agitation with him grow more and more. She repeatedly jabs the knife into the steak.

"No hello to Erica? No, what are you gonna do for Erica? No, just Erica, Erica, Erica."

Reluctantly, Troy concedes and surrenders. "All right. You win."

But Erica in her anger does not hear his concession and continues her ranting. "I don't give a damn about your family."

"You win. Didn't you hear me?"

"Have I? I've sacrificed a lot for you. After this is over, my life will never be the same. I've built a very successful practice, and I'll never be able to practice again."

Troy tries to reassure her that nothing has to change. "Keep your successful practice plus you get what you want—me. Just don't hurt my family," he begs. "Promise me you'll leave them alone."

She studies his face, wondering if his proposal is real. "You would do that, for me? You would sacrifice for me?"

"Yes."

Calmly she traces his lips with her finger. Then she pats his chest over his heart as if she accepts his compassion and believes his sincerity toward her. "I guess I'm a bit of a skeptic. You see, it's that caring you'll always have for them and not for me. You're doing this for them and not for me."

Troy eyes the tapping balls. The clock shows *5:45 p.m.* "I'll do whatever you want. Kiss me."

Erica grows tired of the game playing and the emotional merry-go-round. Deep down, she has convinced herself that he wants her, but her skepticism dominates. "I'm no fool." She adamantly assures him that he will come around, because Jill will be erased permanently from his life. She kisses Troy.

Hopelessness and doom consume Troy. "What do you mean, erased?"

Erica explains that Plan C is in action. She checks the intravenous bag, making sure everything is working properly, but her words and actions puzzle him. She further explains by educating him about her history, revealing more about her upbringing.

"Living with my father gave me a lot of time to read, to experiment. After all, he was a scientist. And like father, like daughter, I became one, too."

"Erica, what kind of experiments?"

"Have you ever heard of ASP?"

"No."

"When it's introduced into your system, first there's vomiting and nausea. Sometimes unstable blood pressure and vision disturbances occur, or you could become disoriented."

"Disoriented?"

"Maybe even comatose. Sometimes death. ASP—amnesic shellfish poisoning."

"Poison? I thought you loved me."

As a scientist, Erica, like her father, worked for the government, but unlike him she was employed by a covert military operation that was responsible for designing and creating highly sophisticated weapons of war. Weapons that affected the mind and could alter or control the mental attributes of the mind. Since she was a psychiatrist who worked in neuroscience, she was the perfect candidate for this kind of work, and of course, her love for scorpions who she learned became very useful only enhanced her experiments. She explained how she made an amazing discovery: the antidote for the sting of a scorpion mixed with domoic acid from parasitic shellfish produced something rather miraculous.

Confusion and bewilderment take hold of Troy, but fear sinks in his stomach.

"I don't understand."

Erica smiles. "Oh, I see fear in your eyes and the best is yet to come." She enlightens him. "Permanent retrograde memory loss. You won't remember yesterday. You won't remember what happens to your family. Then, you really will be mine."

With horror in his heart and repugnance toward her, he concedes, "I said I was yours, and I am."

She sticks a fresh IV needle in his arm. He squints from the slight sting.

"You're a man of honor, and that's a problem."

The solution slowly travels down the IV tubing. He pleads with her again. "Don't do this."

She taps the tubing to hurry the flow. "It'll be over soon."

"Kiss me."

Troy's request surprises Erica. "What?"

"You're right. It's always been you. Kiss me."

Like a puppy desperate for affection and attention, Erica plasters kisses all over Troy's face. He eyes the IV tubing, contemplating a way to stop whatever fate is about to deal him.

Then reality sets in for Erica. The profession she gained notoriety in that garnered national and international recognition for her innovative work in psychology and neuroscience kicks in.

"What do you take me for? You think you can fool me with this act? It doesn't matter. Soon, I'll have your mind and your body."

The solution travels down halfway.

Troy swallows the pain of saying the emotion he doesn't feel. "I...I love you.

"What?"

"I love you. Come here," he says. For he has a plan, too—Plan D, and it's in action.

The IV solution is now about a fourth of the way from entering his body.

"Kiss me, Erica."

Erica leans in closer.

"You go to hell!" he shouts. Troy headbutts her hard. She falls back and knocks the food tray over. The steak knife lands on the side of the bed, and Erica's head hits the edge of the nightstand. She collapses to the floor, unconscious.

Quickly and painfully, he yanks his arm hard, and the IV tubing snaps from his arm, stopping the solution an inch away from entering his body, seconds away from erasing his memory. The IV stand topples over. The knife lands almost on the edge of the blanket about halfway down. Troy stretches trying to grab the knife with his fingers. His fingertips barely touch the knife and push it away.

"Damn! I can do this."

Troy tries again. His fingers crawl to the tip of the knife's handle, and he tries to grab it with two fingers, but it slides. The knife slips closer to the edge of the bed. "God, help me." The swinging ball clock chimes two times. Now, the clock shows *6:00 p.m.* He twists the sheet between his fingers grabbing it and is able to pull the sheet closer to him. The knife rides the bed sheet as he slowly and carefully pulls it closer to him. But again, the knife slips down and turns away from him.

Sweat beads pop up across his face as he strains, stretching for the knife. He struggles as his fingers carefully crawl to the blade of the knife. It almost slips, but this time he grips the knife's blade and squeezes it tight. The blade slits the inside of his fingers. Blood stains the blanket. Troy looks down at Erica to make sure she does not stir. Blood seeps from the gash in her forehead. He is able to maneuver turning the handle around and grabs it. Quickly, he saws through the restraints on one hand, then the other.

Chapter 17

Two Hours Left

FREEDOM AT LAST or almost it appears. The metal locks are still clamped tightly around Troy's wrist which could still signal the nanosensors. He eases off the bed down to Erica who lies unconscious on the floor and begins to hunt through her lab coat pockets carefully. He finds the key, then unlocks the metal bands. Finally, freedom, he has his freedom. The clock chimes and shows 6:00 p.m. Quickly, he snatches the clock from the wall. He relives the torture she has put him through as he stands over Erica's unconscious body. He raises the clock high, ready to bash her head in and put an end to his torment. "You'll never hurt my family or me again."

Angry, he throws it down hard, but the clock smashes next to her head, intentionally. Instead, he pushes the aquarium over, toppling its contents and the scorpions begin to crawl out. How befitting for her demise.

An hour later, a few miles away from the Pendergrass Sanitarium, Troy stands on the curb of a side road, shivering as the rain drenches him and covers the slick street like a shallow creek. Cars and trucks zip past him. Sirens shriek from a distance. Yellow, red, and blue lights glow from the direction of the blaring sirens coming closer and closer to him. Troy runs for cover and jumps in the wooded brush behind him as police cars speed by— lights flash and sirens wail. Oncoming traffic moves to the median, stopping to allow the police cars to race by on the slippery two-lane highway.

After the last police car races past Troy, he runs toward several of the cars that have stopped, hoping to catch a ride but several drivers sped off as Troy approached their cars. The driver of an eighteen wheeler honks his horn. He rushes up to the opened passenger door.

The driver says, "It's raining pretty hard out here. Hop in."

"Thanks." Troy climbs in.

"Where you going?"

"Tarleton." Troy responds.

"Lucky you. I'm going right through there.."

The truck's clock shows 6:30 p.m. Inside his wet pants pocket is the remote. Slyly, Troy pulls it out a little so as not to alarm the driver. The remote has now converted to a timer. The countdown is set one hour and thirty minutes, a minute passes, then, one hour and twenty-nine minutes left to disarm the bomb inside of the lookalike.

The truck passes a sign that shows Tarleton, fifty miles away. "Not far now," the driver says to a shivering Troy. He reaches behind him in the open cabin area of the truck and grabs a towel. "Here, try this. That ought to take the chill off." He tosses the towel over to Troy.

Drenched and shivering, Troy wipes his anguished face. Time is running out, but maybe his luck has finally changed. "Think you can go a little faster," Troy says to the driver.

Chapter 18

ONE HOUR

JILL HANGS ONE of Troy's shirts in the bedroom closet from a clothes basket. Her duplicitous husband sneaks up on her and grabs Jill from behind. He whispers in her ear, "Game night."

"Ok, in a minute."

Downstairs, Madi waits for her parents at the dining table to join her in a game of Monopoly, their Friday night family ritual. Jill walks up, and the synthetic emotionless replica of Troy follows behind and pats her on the butt. He mimics that gesture well and remarks romantically, "The winner gets first choice of whatever he or she wants her mate to do."

"Anything?"

"Anything," he reiterates.

"Then get ready for second place." Jill says with much confidence.

"Hmm, winning works both ways," the lookalike chuckles.

Madi chimes in, "I don't know what the first and second place mean, but if it has anything to do with this game, then both of you get ready to lose. And when I win, I can stay up till midnight on a school night at Rose's."

The imposter looks toward Jill. "You want to be the bad guy on this one, Jill?" He hops up and exits to the kitchen.

"That's not on the table for discussion or betting."

"No fair, Mom."

Troy comes back to the table from the kitchen and sits down. Madi pleads with her father to help her out. "Ok, Dad, I need you to give Mom instructions on Sex 101, 102, and maybe 103. You know, sweet talk her. Convince her to see the bigger picture about extending my curfew."

"Oh, no you didn't go there." Jill responds.

The feigned double quickly assumes the role and adds, "Stop while you're ahead, young lady. The best we'll do is 11:30 p.m., and only on a Friday or Saturday. Now, let's play."

"I'm sixteen." Madi stubbornly responds.

"And?"

"I've matured."

Jill chimes in, "And I think you've forgotten how your behavior and grades have been over the year. So table it. No more discussion."

"Ok, I concede. Like my new word?" Madi adds.

Jill responds, "This is called parenting, and I'm the boss. Like my word?"

"Ok boss, we get the picture," her husband says. "Let's play."

AT THE SANITARIUM, the two CNAs rush in to rescue Erica from the scorpions. One CNA stomps the scorpions while another carries Erica toward the door for safety. Then, another charges in with a pesticide container and starts spraying some of the scorpions, killing them. But Erica comes to and sees her family, her pet scorpions die, which angers her tremendously.

She pushes the CNA aside and takes the pesticide sprayer from him, then sprays the remaining poisonous solution on him, but only a little dispenses. He inhales the chemical causing him to gag and choke. The solution fills his nostrils and takes over his lungs. He collapses to his knees.

"Oh, you're not gonna die, but you will pay for this." Erica bashes his head with the container, knocking him out.

Chapter 19

TIME'S UP

STILL DARKNESS. TROY emerges from the dark shadows of the evening and runs up to a window of his house. He peeps in to find the synthetic mirror image engaged in a game of Monopoly with Jill and Madi. His heart rips as he watches him take his place during their family bonding time.

When the lookalike throws the dice, Jill makes a comment about the large bandage covering his hand. She grabs at it. "Sweetheart, what happened?"

Being a sarcastic prick, he says, "Oh, I'm sweetheart now?"

She runs her fingers over the bandage and starts peeling it back. Quickly, Troy snatches his hand away explaining that the little furry critter, Fifi, bit him. "It's a minor bite," he says. He wants to conceal what's under the bandage and put aside any suspicions she might have, but Jill is concerned and not easily dissuaded.

"That's an awfully big bandage to simply be nothing. Let me look at it."

He insists, "It's just a scratch. Nothing."

The truth of the matter is that the metal ligaments and wires inside his robotic body would be exposed revealing the horrendous lie.

"Really, it's nothing. I'd better check on the popcorn."

The microwave timer beeps, and the double quickly moves toward the kitchen. "Popcorn coming right up." He leaves Jill somewhat baffled.

Madi yells out to her dad, "Load it up with lots of butter, Dad."

Troy watches the loves of his life through the window, his wife and daughter laughing and talking with one they think is him, a stranger, a killer, not knowing that their demise is only minutes away.

Madi yells, "Dad, where's the popcorn? Hurry up! It's 7:40 p.m. C'mon, so we can finish the game." While waiting for him, Madi pulls her cell phone out and checks her Facebook. "Mom, you want to see how my class project is doing?"

"Sure, baby."

Madi shows her mother the Facebook site that displays a 3D bar graph depicting where each student ranks. The vertical axis shows the top ten ranking. The horizontal axis shows the voting count. Madi ranks third.

Jill commends her. "Number three. Impressive."

"But I need more votes. Did you call Aunt Vi? With that slew of hers, I'm an automatic winner, or at least I could move to second place."

The fact that it's 7:40 p.m. intensifies Troy's desperation. He has twenty minutes to save his family, twenty minutes to save the woman and daughter whom he loves, twenty minutes to stop Erica's treacherous plan from becoming a deadly reality.

While the lookalike is out of sight in the kitchen, Troy digs through the muddy earth beneath him and finds several small rocks. He throws them at the window trying to get Jill's attention. Jill looks around but thinks she's hearing things and resumes playing.

The rain drenches Troy as he urgently hunts for more small rocks in the earth below him. He finds a couple more and throws them at the window. Again, Jill follows the sound, trying to determine where it is coming from. She looks toward the window.

"Did you hear that, Madi?"

"No, Mom, it won't work." Madi moves her game piece on the board.

Jill is baffled by her response. "What are you talking about?"

"Mom, you're trying to distract me."

Jill insists, "I heard something."

Madi is confident that the game is her win. "Your attempt to distract me is not gonna work. I'm not gonna lose."

The imposter returns with a bowl of popcorn. "Distracted, my angels?"

Madi is certain that Jill is trying to use this distraction as a ploy to win the game, or else she's having an MLC moment. "Mom's hearing things. She thought she heard a noise at the window."

"I did hear something. Humor me, darling, and go check it out."

The double crosses over to the window, and Troy ducks down. The synthetic sheath of a figure looks out, then down, but he doesn't see Troy hiding beneath the windowsill in the bushes. His eyes change to X-ray vision, scoping the yard. The only thing his X-ray eyes see is the skeleton outline of two frogs hopping from a tree to the other side of the yard.

The phone rings.

Jill answers the phone. "Hello." She frowns as she listens to the other party on the line. "It's for you—the other woman." Except for his present behavior, in twenty years, he has never given her a reason to doubt his faithfulness to her. So, Jill doesn't read too much into this. She smiles and passes the phone to her husband.

He kisses at Jill as he takes the phone from her. "You know there's no one else. Who would go through this headache with you?"

She finds no humor in his remark and snatches the phone back.

"Kidding, I'm just kidding." The double grabs the phone and lays a sweet kiss on Jill's lips.

Jill chastises him about his midlife-crisis-personality disorder and urges him to see a doctor or psychologist to help him deal with the issue, because she has grown tired of his up and down mood swings.

"I'm not trying to become a divorce court statistic," she responds, "but you are pushing my buttons."

The lookalike ignores her ranting and listens to the caller. "No." He listens more. "When? Got it."

Madi rolls the dice and moves her game piece. "I win!" She shouts and explodes with excitement. "Great game, Mom and Dad. While you two have been teetering around divorce, you gave me the upper hand to beat you. Good job, parents. Like my new word, teetering, Dad?"

The fake dad responds, "Sunshine, keep that up and next, you'll be running this country. You're getting better and better."

Troy listens at the window. Hearing his nemesis call his daughter Sunshine grips his heart and tears at him even more. He searches for a weapon, something to destroy his enemy with. He finds a broken piece of plumbing pipe jutting out and partially covered under the earth beneath him. He digs it up.

Meanwhile, Jill interrupts the father and daughter fun banter. She hops up. "Well, that's it for me." She heads toward the back to her art studio, but not before giving Madi a hug.

The imposter snaps his fingers gesturing to Madi and Jill to wait before going in their different directions. They hesitate and wait for him to end his phone conversation. He completes the call and hugs them then takes a selfie of the three of them. He kisses them on the forehead and tries to win Jill's favor.

"I'm sorry."

"For what?" Madi asks.

"His narcissistic erratic behavior," Jill says.

"I promise I'll do better."

"See the doctor?"

"I'll make an appointment on Monday."

A moment of truce, Jill kisses him and they embrace. She rubs his back caressing him and pulls him tighter in her arms.

Madi, embarrassed, says, "Ok, ok, ok. That's it for me, too. I don't need to learn Sex Education 101, 102, 103, whatever, watching my parents make out. I'm going over to Rose's to finish up the presentation for our forensic art project." She trots up the stairs to get her books. The clock on the wall over the fireplace mantel chimes five minutes before eight.

Troy's eyes water as he watches the love of his life kissing another man, this horrid machine whom she seems so comfortable with.

Madi comes back down the stairs. "Bye, parents."

Jill exercises her parental authority. "Be back at ten thirty."

"Eleven," Madi counters.

"Ten thirty, like your mother said, " the double adds.

Madi kisses them both and dashes out the front door but not before confirming, "See ya' at ten thirty."

Jill exits to the studio, and the imposter crosses back over to the window looking out, searching. Then, he leaves the room.

While his daughter may be safe, Troy questions his ability to save his wife. Fear for her safety gnaws at him knowing that the humanlike replica covers a synthetic monster underneath, a walking time bomb.

Three Minutes And Thirty Seconds Before 8:00 p.m.

Troy tries to pry the window open but with no success. It's locked. He creeps around the house to another window and tries opening it. Again, no success.

Three Minutes Before 8:00 p.m.

Troy runs to the fence, but it is locked from the inside, and time is not on his side. He runs to the sliding glass door next to the kitchen. Success, it opens. Quietly, he eases into the kitchen and looks to see if the imposter is anywhere around. No imposter and time is running out. The timer inside the remote shows three minutes remaining. Quietly, he hunts through a drawer. "The wire cutters, where are they? They should be here." Troy searches through another drawer and still no wire cutters, then another. He ferrets through the papers inside. The wire cutters are hiding under some surveys. Countdown, one minute left for him to stop the bomb from exploding. Three wires—red, yellow, and green keep the bomb's timer going only seconds away before exploding. SNIP. He cuts the green wire.

Thirty Seconds Before 8:00 p.m.

Jill works in her studio. She hammers colorful indentations into a metal sheet creating another work of art.

Ten Seconds Before 8:00 p.m.

Jill layers colors of spray paint on her sheet metal creation. She dips the hammer into a different color and hammers into the sheet metal, finishing the silhouette outline of a beautiful woman with child. The colors run into each other across her pregnant stomach to show a mixture of colors—an abstract. A clock hanging on the wall reads 8:00 p.m.

She is about to hammer again when a disturbing shattering sound comes from inside the house. GLASS BREAKS. The house trembles like a train derailing.

She rushes in with the hammer to find her husband pinned on the ground wrestling with another man on the floor but his face is not visible to her. Jill thinks the man is an intruder.

On the floor, Troy is on top of his synthetic nemesis choking him with the pipe pressed against his neck hoping this might damage something in his robotic system. Jill yells fearing for her love's life. "Oh, my God, Troy!" She rushes over to help who she thinks is her husband. Jill is about to hammer the intruder when he looks up at her and screams. "Jill! It's me!"

"What!" Jill stunned by whom she sees drops the hammer. Is she seeing double? Are her eyes playing tricks on her? Could she be imagining things? The intruder looks like Troy.

The imposter pushes the pipe from his neck and tosses it aside. He punches Troy in the mouth, spinning him down to the floor. Jill, still in shock and uncertain of who is who, stares back and forth at both of them. "Troy? I mean—what the hell? I mean, who the hell are you and you?"

The two continue fighting. Troy bounces back up and quickly reverts to his fighting skills acquired during his previous counter intelligence operative days. He karate kicks his nemesis hard in the chest sending him across the room, bashing him into the wall.

The lookalike yells, "It's me, Jill!"

Troy repeats, "No, Jill, he's lying, I'm Troy."

Jill is so confused. She looks back and forth at them, trying to decipher this duplicitous DNA coding.

The fight becomes more intense. Troy grabs a chair and hits the synthetic double over the head. It has little impact, but he stumbles. The chair breaks into pieces. The lookalike backhands Troy and punches him several times in the face. The blows to his face splatter blood all over Troy.

The double calls out, "Jill!"

Jill applies her Aikido techniques and kicks Troy hard in the side, sending him sliding across the floor. He grabs his side in pain. She runs over to hit Troy with what she thinks will be the final blow, a butt in the throat with the heel of her palm, but she hesitates, looking down at the man who looks like the man she loves. That moment of doubt may have saved his life. She stops.

Troy holds his side and cries out in great pain, "I love you, Jill." Barely able to speak, he mutters the words again, "I love you..."

"What?"

"He's not real. He's not me. He's a synthetic monster created to look like me."

The double stammers. "No, no, no, don't listen to him. I'm your husband."

"Now, I want you to listen. I was kidnapped by a woman who created this thing. He was created to destroy you. There was a bomb inside of him, in his eyes."

"A bomb!"

"But I was able to stop it. I cut the wires in the remote."

"Nonsense. Who are you going to believe? He broke into our house."

"I'm only trying to protect you. I promise." Troy pulls the remote out from his pocket. The back is open exposing the cut green wire.

Jill is torn between two men, one her real husband and the other, a false imitation. Her mind fades back to earlier that night when she noticed Troy's hand was covered with a bandage. She remembered how he was very protective of his hand and would not allow her to see the cut.

"Let me see your hand." She demands.

The double nervously responds, "What? Why?"

"Show me your hand! Remember you said Fifi's bite was nothing. Your hand," she insists.

He bows his head looking down at the bandaged hand. Then, a cynical smile crosses his face. He rises like a tall pillar lifting Troy's broken body and using him to shield the view of his now white eyes to Jill. He lifts Troy's body over his head and with great force throws him sailing across the room smashing into the dining room table. BAM. Troy's badly beaten body hits the edge of the table hard toppling over on it. The impact sends the

Monopoly game sitting on the table flying across the floor, scattering the board and playing pieces.

Troy is badly hurt. He moans in pain. "Oh-h-h-h-h-h."

Jill sees the truth, what is not real—white eyes.

"No! No! No!" She screams in horror.

The angry lookalike charges toward her and grabs her by the throat, squeezing tighter and tighter. Her strength fades away as he almost squeezes the life out of her.

Troy, defenseless against this robotic force struggles to pull himself up and falls on one knee holding his arm. With little fight left, he manages to gain enough strength to stand up.

"This is my family...and I want him back!" He barrels into the replica. Jill drops to the floor. Both men land on the floor with Troy on top. But the inanimate lookalike is unstoppable. He dangles Troy like a puppet on a string as he rises to his feet choking him.

Out of nowhere, Erica rushes in. "Down! Put him down!"

Gripping anger seems to control the object of destruction that Erica created, or has he reprogrammed himself so that he is in control. Troy gags from the choking.

"Stop! Put him down! Erica commands.

The imposter succumbs to her commands. His eyes change back to normal. He stops choking Troy and drops him hard on the floor.

Jill crawls over to Troy and embraces him. His bruised and bloody body is covered with deep gashes. She brushes his hair from his face and wipes the blood from his mouth.

Watching Jill embrace and care for Troy infuriates Erica. "No, he belongs to me!" Erica hits herself hard in the chest like a predator having satisfaction and control over its defenseless prey. "It's him and me—and you keep getting in my way."

Troy pleads with her to stop this madness, but Erica grows impatient. She starts her nervous habit of clawing her neck until skin breaks and blood seeps out. She claws deeper as tears well in her eyes, not from the pain of the wounds she's created, but from the wounds of a broken heart.

She cries, "You...you said you loved me." Blood slowly drips down and stains her white lab coat. "You promised to love me, but you protect her."

Troy cuts his angry eyes at Erica. "You're sick. You're crazy."

"Crazy? Why are you being so hateful to me?" She turns her anger to Jill. "You did this. You meddling cunt. Always getting in the way. Kill her."

"Get out of here Jill! Run!" Troy yells.

Jill runs, but the synthetic replica blocks her stride and backhands her hard across the face, knocking her down to the floor.

Troy dives at him locking his arm around his neck. He whispers in his ear, "This is the last time you will ever hurt my wife. The next stop for you is the junk yard, you fucking piece of scrap metal." He grips the robot's throat tightly with the crook of his arm. But the robot headbutts Troy from behind in the face, then rams him hard into a cabinet against the wall. Troy's frail body is no match against his robotic strength. He collapses to the floor.

Erica screams at Jill. "You did this!" She lunges toward her, but Jill stops her with an Aikido foot chop to the stomach. Erica crouches holding her stomach. She pulls a small case out of her pocket and opens it. Inside, two syringes lie side by side.

"Never cross a woman in love. Sleeping beauty, it's time for your mind to take a permanent nap. Hold her," she commands the double.

Jill readies herself for the next round. "You're never going to get away with this."

Erica is overly confident. "Oh, but I am."

The imposter's eyes turn white as he inches closer to Jill, who slowly backs away. She eyes the hammer on the floor and grabs it, then swings it at him. But he catches her hand gripping it tightly until she drops the hammer. Then, he backhands her with a hard blow to the face. Erica comes up behind Jill and whacks her over the head with an empty wine bottle knocking Jill unconscious. Jill slides down the wall and collapses on the floor.

"Now to finish this." Erica proceeds to inject Jill in the neck but Troy comes to and dives in between them.

<hr />

A COUPLE OF hours later, the kitchen door slams. The kitchen wall clock shows 10:30 p.m. Madi yells from the kitchen, "I'm home."

There is complete silence throughout the house. She quickly runs upstairs and does not notice her mom lying unconscious on the floor in the family room.

She yells from the top of the stairs as she gets to her room. "And I'm on time!" Still silence. "Hmmm, they must be asleep. Sex 101 must have worn them out."

Madi tiptoes over to her parents' bedroom with her hands covering her eyes. Quietly, she eases their bedroom door open and pokes her head in. She peeks through an opened slit through her fingers so as not to see them in the act. Instead, she finds a dark and empty bedroom. The bed made and not slept in. Madi, somewhat baffled, uncovers her eyes and eases the door shut. "Hmmm."

She rushes back downstairs to the family room. She screams at the sight—her mother's limp body lying on the floor. Horrified, Madi rushes over to her.

"Mom! Mom!" Madi gets no reaction. She shakes her again, but Jill still does not move. Madi fearing the worse, "Please, please, I can't lose you, too." She shakes Jill more, and her eyes open.

Jill swings at Madi, flailing her arms, fighting. Madi grabs her mother's arms to calm her.

"Mom, Mom, it's me, Madi!"

Jill calms down for a second, but her memory goes back to the minutes and seconds when she was fighting for her life. She panics. "Your dad. Where's your dad?"

Madi is scared. "I don't know, Mom. He's not here." She drills her mother. "What happened?

Jill, frantic, calls the police to report her husband missing.

Chapter 20

THE TRUTH

AMBULANCE SIRENS WAIL as they approach the house. The front of the house is a crime scene of unmarked and black and white police cars. Different car lights flash bright yellow, blue, and red hues. Crime scene tape bars the front yard. Police are all around the house, inside and out.

Inside, plainclothes and uniformed police attempt to examine a room that shows no evidence of a struggle or disruption. It is totally clean, almost spotless. Some dust for fingerprints, and others swab for blood samples from the walls, tables, and other furniture. Jill sits in Troy's favorite recliner in the family room, talking with Detective Shameus. She strokes the arms of the chair up and down as if they were really Troy's arms.

Detective Shameus, a veteran officer of thirty-something years in his mid-fifties, is frustrated with life and very impatient. The fact that he is also experiencing MLC doesn't make matters any better for his temperament. He sits on the arm of the recliner looking down at Jill, a bit unorthodox and erratic for professional behavior. He nervously taps an e-cigarette on a cigarette case, a habit that has become his substitute anti-depressant pill.

Jill collapses in tears, burying her head in her hands. It's not Detective Shameus' nature to be patient, so he taps his anti-depressant substitute on the case.

"Come on out with it."

"I'm trying." She barks back.

"Now, let's go over this again. What happened?"

Jill frantically tries to explain. "They, no the woman kidnapped my husband. I believe she was a doctor."

"What makes you think that?"

"Well, if the fact that she tried to stab me with a medical syringe isn't convincing enough, then I don't know what is."

"I see and you say her accomplice was a robot who looked like your husband."

But Detective Shameus questions the facts when Madi contradicts everything about her missing father. She describes the past few months, leading up to conversations with a man whom she thought was her real father and very present in her life, her mother's debut gala art exhibition, their celebrated twentieth wedding anniversary tango at the exhibition, and of course, tonight's family game night. So how could her husband not be present when Madi just contradicted Jill's story?

He questions Jill one more time. "You say your husband was kidnapped."

Jill, perturbed and upset, says, "Yes! How many times must I tell you? You need me to draw you a picture? While you stand here questioning the validity of this, he could be hurt. Or worse, dead."

"Ok, ok, ok. Let's say I believe you. So who was the guy who's been here or never left that your daughter refers to as her father and keeps talking about? Tell me, who was that?"

"A robot."

"Robot? Original, I'll say that for you." Detective Shameus scratches his head and taps his antidepressant e-cigarette even harder. "That's your story, and you're sticking to it?"

"Yes! He had these white eyes and a bomb on him—no, inside of him that was supposed to go off. But my husband was able to stop the bomb from exploding."

Detective Shameus, amazed at this fantastic story, says, "Wow! What a fabrication. What an imagination. Kept—key word—that's probably been the most sensible thing you've said all night. Your husband was a kept man for another woman's pleasure."

Madi interrupts and slices into the detective, "My father would never look at another woman, let alone be 'kept'!"

Detective Shameus' lack of confidence in Jill's story upsets her tremendously, and likewise, he grows more and more impatient with her. He puts the e-cigarette to his mouth, but before he can light up, she stops him. "This is a smoke-free house."

"They're electronic, the cigarettes—no tobacco, only vapor.

"What?"

"Vapor, and that's what this whole fabrication of a story sounds like—nothing but air."

"What!"

He points to several empty wine bottles standing on the bar and asks, "Sure that's not the problem?"

She resents him questioning her sobriety and insists that he should be out looking for them—looking for the woman, the man—no, the robot.

"Stop right there," says Detective Shameus. "That's where you're not making any sense." Detective Shameus taps the e-cigarette on the case again.

Frustrated and frantic, Jill repeats herself. "They kidnapped him. And…and she created a robot that looked like Troy, who I thought was my husband."

Detective Shameus rolls his eyes in disbelief. "Whoa, confusing."

His female counterpart shadowing him interrupts and beckons for him. They chat for a few minutes, then he returns to Jill, nervously tapping the e-cigarette on the cigarette case.

"We've finished dusting the place. No other fingerprints were found—just yours."

Jill says, "This is absurd. Are you being impertinent just for the hell of it? I'm telling you, they were here."

He replies, "Are you sure the wine isn't talking?" He eyes the empty wine bottles on the bar again. "I can't make any sense of this."

"You don't believe me. Then where did this blood come from?" She touches the dried blood from a cut on her head.

"Perhaps after you had a little too much to drink, you fell and hit your head on something." Detective Shameus is skeptical and questions her story even more; there are so many holes. "Ok, there is the absence of any bodies. There was a Troy. He's not a twin. And to top it off, you say he was not real, but a robot. Where's the proof? A fantastic story."

Jill becomes hysterical and bursts out in tears. Madi rushes over to comfort her mother. "Mom, what's wrong?"

"Mr. Detective here seems to think your dad was cheating on me, and I'm making all this up because I'm a drunk—or even worse, I got rid of the bodies."

"My mom's telling the truth. My dad wouldn't look at another woman. Except for his MLC—"

Detective Shameus finishes her sentence. "Midlife crisis, I see. That answers a lot, and I gather you're going through the same thing, Mrs. Norton. I call it the other PMS, pre-menopause syndrome, which might explain your questionable behavior."

"Questionable?" asks Jill.

He confesses his discontent with his own life because of the effects of MLC. "You know, I ended a twenty-five year marriage to the best woman I've ever known. Now, I have a wife twenty years my junior, started a new family with two young kids, two and four—"

"—Chief." His female counterpart tries to control him with no success.

Detective Shameus taps the e-cigarette case harder and harder. "And a third on the way. Yep, now how old are you?"

Jill sarcastically reproves him. "Women go through menopause."

Detective Shameus says, "Same thing."

Madi attempts to stop this fruitless banter. "My dad loves me—us."

But Detective Shameus is in rare form. "I love my grown children, too."

Trying to control his surly didactic behavior, the female detective calls out to him, "Chief."

Detective Shameus sighs. "Yeah, MLC can be a bitch."

The female detective calls out again, "Chief!"

Jill, now very impatient, scolds him about his duty to paying taxpayers and he tries to help her understand the process. "Missing persons are not investigated before twenty-four hours have passed. The premises are immaculate. There's no evidence of any kind of a struggle and let's not forget, Troy was here."

Detective Shameus says to Jill, "Mrs. Norton...can I call you Jill?"

"No. Mrs. Norton."

"Ok, Mrs, Norton. Again, it hasn't been twenty-four hours yet."

"I see," Jill says. "You're not gonna help." She crosses over to the front door and opens it.

Detective Shameus responds, "Look these are tough economic times, and I can't justify the manpower on what sounds like a jealous, alcohol-induced whim."

This infuriates her. "Jealous? Alcohol-induced! Leave!"

Detective Shameus calls it quits for his team, and they all exit. As they leave, the female detective ushers Detective Shameus out, arm-locking him and scolding him about sharing too much. "TMI, Detective Shameus, TMI."

Jill slams the door so hard, she almost knocks it off the hinges. She's weary, scared, and worried consumed with frustration and despair. She sits down in the recliner, caressing and stroking the recliner arm as if she was making love to Troy.

Madi sits on the other arm of the chair and leans over to hug her mother. Jill looks into her daughter's eyes.

"I don't know what to do."

Madi hesitates, afraid to ask the unthinkable but does. "Do you think Daddy's ali—" and is interrupted before she can finish her words.

"No, don't say it," Jill insists. "We're gonna find him. We're going to find him."

Jill kisses Madi's forehead. They embrace, holding one another to provide the only support they seem to have—each other.

Chapter 21

AND THIS IS 'CAUSE I LOVE YOU

HOURS LATER AND miles away from Georgia, a car travels down a narrow two-lane road surrounded by woods and covered with patches of melted snow that peek through the brown earth, a remnant unusual for this time of year. It's late March; the dogwood trees are just about to blossom with the beautiful pink and white flowers trailing alongside the narrow lanes. Soon the wooded area will smell of pine from the trees that sprout tall and the aromatic cinnamon scent of white dogwood petals down the Fairlane Dogwood Trail pathway. It's been an Indian summer, an unexpected cold snap, then the warming spell, an effect of global warming. It changes things.

Erica slowly cruises down the secluded and narrow road. She stops. Troy, still unconscious, slumps next to her in the passenger's seat. She says over her shoulder, "You should have killed her." With a hard stare through the rearview mirror, she looks back at her creation.

"Remember, I couldn't."

Her mind retraces the scene in Troy's trashed family room hours earlier.

The double squeezed Jill's hand so tight until she dropped the hammer. Erica lunged at her with the syringe, but Troy dove between the two, and the syringe emptied into his neck. He collapsed to the floor.

The thought that she might have caused harm to Troy when her intended victim was Jill gnawed at her and changed to an almost uncontrollable rage. She grabbed one of the wine bottles and cracked it over Jill's head, knocking her unconscious. She screamed at Jill lying on the floor.

"This was supposed to happen to you! This was to wipe you completely out of his life!"

She ordered the lookalike, "Take him to the car while I clean things up and finish your mess." He threw Troy over his shoulder and exited, while Erica dumped everything into a trash bag. She wiped clean all traces of her fingerprints and the blood spattered around the room.

As she went back to the kitchen sink, she passed a set of carving knives sitting in a knife stand. She grabbed a knife and had a fleeting thought, contemplating how to end what stood between a love for life and herself. As she crouched over Jill, she ripped the blouse open over her heart. "I am going to end this now, my trophy." Then she touched the knife to Jill's skin, ready to carve what was standing between her and the love she'd waited and longed for. "Never again will you or anyone come between us."

Before Erica could do the unthinkable, the synthetic double grabbed Erica's hand. "No, not now!"

The interruption angered Erica. "What? Then *you* kill her."

"Sirens—don't you hear them?"

His computerized topography zeroed in on several police cars rushing toward the house. A virtual ETA flashes fifteen minutes away several times.

Erica heard nothing. "There are no sirens." She continued her butchering attempt but was halted by the faint sound of police sirens in the distance. She listened. Louder and louder. Closer and closer. Erica and the double rushed out.

Now Erica sits in the car and looks over at Troy, sleeping peacefully in his unconscious state. She runs her fingers through his wavy locks. "We're together now."

Erica commands the double, "C'mon, help me." She goes to the trunk of the car and pulls out a mallet. "Cover him. Make sure you cover his face."

The lookalike obeys Erica's every command. She's nervous and hesitates, pacing back and forth before walking around to the passenger side.

"This is for us," she says to Troy.

Then she bashes the windshield in on Troy. Glass shatters everywhere, inside the car and all over his limp body. Shards of glass rip through the blanket. Blood seeps through the blanket in several places.

Finally, she takes a piece of the shattered glass and carves a line across her upper arm cringing in pain. "Uhhhh." Blood runs down her arm.

She hands the lookalike another set of car keys. "I'll see you later."

He quickly travels through the woods to another car hidden on an out of the way trail and calls 911. He drives off.

Meanwhile, Erica slides back into the driver's seat and rest her head for a moment agonizing over the tumultuous events that transpired just a few hours ago up to now. Troy's body slumps over on her, and she embraces him. She kisses his forehead then his lips so passionately and starts the car.

"And this is 'cause I love you." Erica presses her foot to the pedal and accelerates, then quickly rolls out of the car.

BAM! The car rams into a huge tree. The airbag expands, and Troy's head bangs up against the dash-board. He lands over the top through the shattered window.

Chapter 22

CHANGE, A NEW LIFE

SIRENS BLARE FROM ambulances racing to the emergency entrance at New Life General Hospital. Inside, several nurses and doctors rush Troy's bloody body through the corridors. Blood seeps through the bandaging wrapped around his head. Erica rushes alongside the gurney when a nurse rushes over to tend to her arm as Troy groggily comes to and cries out in pain.

Erica brushes the nurse off and insists that she take care of Troy and not her. The nurse then diverts her attention to him.

"Do you know who you are?" the nurse asks.

"I'm...," Troy mumbles, stumbling over his words and Erica finishes his sentence.

"...Troy, Troy Miller."

The nurse bluntly asks, "And you are?"

"Mrs. Miller, his wife." Finally, Erica hears the words she so very much longed for—an uncanny bliss.

Moments later Troy lies asleep in bed with his head rebandaged and hooked to several beeping monitors and an IV. Erica stands over him. A small town doctor enters to attend to him, with the nurse following behind.

The doctor flashes a penlight into each eye. "Um-m-m. Now, what exactly happened?"

Erica explains. "We were on our way home, and I lost control of the car." She buries her face in her hands, pretending to cry. "I was driving too fast."

The doctor continues his examination and checks Troy from head to toe.

Erica asks, "Doctor, what's your prognosis? Is he gonna be all right?"

"He sustained major head trauma and a concussion, but physically, he's going to be fine."

Somewhat groggy, Troy awakens. The doctor continues, "But he may not…"

"…may…not…what?" Troy mumbles in a great deal of pain as he struggles to sit up.

"Remember. Take it easy now." the doctor replies.

"Remember?"

"With that concussion, your memory was probably affected, and you won't remember."

Erica smiles but quickly suppresses that expression. After all she is responsible for his injuries. She rushes to him and hugs him.

"Oh, honey, I'm so sorry."

"For what? Where am I?"

"New Life General Hospital." The doctor answers.

Erica anxiously interjects, "I'm your wife and there was an accident. You had a bad head injury." She studies his face to see his reaction for she doesn't know how he will receive the news.

Troy says to her, "I'm not trying to hurt you, but I don't know you."

The doctor shakes his head. "And I'm sorry to say that you have amnesia."

Troy shocked, echoes, "Amnesia."

The doctor further explains, "Retrograde amnesia. The impact you sustained traumatized your brain with severe memory damage. You can remember basic things, but have no memory of your past."

"I should have been more careful," Erica says sorrowfully.

The doctor reassures them both that his memory could come back.

"Come back? What? Come back!" Suddenly, Erica, disturbed by the doctor's prognosis, has a panic attack; her breathing becomes a bit erratic.

The doctor attempts to attend to her, but she shoves him off.

"Water, I…I just need some water." She starts coughing all the way to the bathroom and shuts the door. She rants to herself, "No, no, no, no, no, no, no. Come back? No, no, no, no. Come back!"

The doctor knocks on the door. "Mrs. Miller…Mrs. Miller, are you all right?"

"I'm all right." After all, she knows what the drug will do, since she developed this experimental concoction. Erica returns to Troy's bedside, calm now.

The doctor, disturbed by her agitated temperament, pacifies her. "It's not as bad as you think, Mrs. Miller. Another sudden traumatic head injury, you never know, could bring his memory back. The good thing is you can help him rebuild his life."

Hearing that excites Erica. She smiles, "It'll be like starting all over again…huh, Doc?"

"Yes, starting a new life."

Erica beams. Troy, bewildered, is concerned.

Chapter 23

DISCOVERY

Madi sits on the floor in the family room thumbing through the pages of Troy's college yearbook. She stops on the who's who page and reads a caption over a picture of Erica shabbily dressed with a bird's nest hairdo and unflattering cat eyeglasses. *Not likely to succeed in career and definitely unlikely to succeed in love.* She chuckles and flips to the cheerleaders' page.

Jill enters the room carrying a tray of sandwiches, glasses, and a pitcher of iced lemonade. She serves her daughter.

"Any luck, Madi?"

"No. Any one of these could fit the description you gave me, Mom, any of them."

Madi flips through the cheerleader pictures again and returns to Erica's picture staring at it. "Well, maybe not all of them." She turns the page then takes a bite of a sandwich. "The brunettes are beautiful."

The cheerleaders page shows a mix of beautiful brunettes and blondes, all ethnicities. "Mom, they're all beautiful."

Jill sits in the recliner and views the yearbook with Madi.

She sips her drink. "You're right, they are, and I can't imagine any of them being involved in this. None of them look like the woman who attacked me."

"Are you sure, Mom? Look again."

Jill looks over the page again, tracing the outline of their frames with her fingers.

"No. Nothing, nothing stands out about any of them."

"Mom, what if—"

"—what if what, sweetheart?

"Suppose we don't find dad a..."

"... don't? It just means we've got our work cut out for us. One of them is the key. I know it."

Troy gets out of the car and slams the door, which irritates Erica. She has a very short fuse and fusses, "Don't take the car door off!"

Her reaction seemed somewhat strange and abnormal, a bit over the top. He has mixed feelings about her quick temper. Then he looks around his new surroundings, a beautiful upscale ski lodge styled home nestled in the middle of no man's land in a secluded wooded area. It is located high up in the hills where traces of winter are more visible. Unmelted snow covers the tall pine trees and brown earth. For a brief moment, the solitude gives him peace and security, but that is short-lived as reality sets in. Chilly vapor blows from his mouth when he talks.

"Still quiet. I have no recollection, no inclination—I don't remember any of this."

"Darling, it's alright." Erica's reassuring words somewhat comfort him.

"But I remember nothing."

"The good thing is, I do. It's like the doctor said. I'll be here to help you remember everything. We're starting all over again."

"You're so patient with me." He smiles. Troy appreciates the supportive charade Erica displays, a make-believe facade that eases some of her worries and frustrations.

Erica leans in to kiss Troy on the lips, but he quickly dismisses that intimacy and pecks her on the cheek. This is all so much for him to grasp—a life that he knows nothing about past and present and a wife who in the mix of this is a stranger that expects him to perform like a robot, his husbandly duties. He shivers, rubbing his hands together and blowing whatever warm air he has on them. "It's cold out here. I guess we'd better get inside."

They quickly grab their belongings from the car and rush up to the door.

Troy asks, "We're starting all over again, right?

"Yes," she answers.

Troy sweeps Erica off of her feet and carries her over the threshold. An odd question comes to Troy as they enter their home. "Do we have any pets?"

An aquarium sits in a corner of the contemporary decorated living room. Framed photos of Troy and Erica embracing line several bookshelves, depicting a history of what appears to be two people deeply in love. From the past to the present are pictures of them embracing on romantic getaways, cruises, at gala affairs, and many different settings.

He studies a photo sitting on the fireplace mantel while Erica excuses herself to the bedroom.

"I'm going to get comfortable. Wanna join me?"

Troy smiles briefly as he crosses over to the bedroom door, but does not follow her inside. He stops at the bedroom doorway. Instead, he stops and blows a kiss at her. She catches it to her heart and leaves the door ajar when she enters.

As he looks at the pictures throughout the room, he mumbles, "Lots of pictures of us, but no children. None."

"What was that?"

"There are no children in any of these pictures."

Erica calls out, "Ummm, we decided to wait."

With mixed feelings and somewhat puzzled Troy asks, "How long have we been waiting?"

Erica comes out of the bedroom in sexy lingerie. She responds as she goes to the kitchen, "How long have we been waiting? Twenty years."

"So how long have we been married?"

"Twenty years."

The timeframe seems questionable to Troy, now even more perplexed. "Huh, long time and no children."

Erica explains that they both decided to wait because of the business.

"So, what do I do?"

"You...we own a rare exotic pet store.

Surprised, Troy says, "Me? Rare exotic pets? I've always done that?"

"Yes."

Troy was more and more inquisitive. "Where's our shop?"

"In town."

"What town?"

Erica starts making a sandwich spreading dressing on it and grows more irritated with Troy's quizzing her. In her frustration, she slaps layer after layer of deli meat on the bread. She's created a mountainous pile wrought with nervousness from his questions.

"Where are we?" He persist.

She becomes more agitated with all the questions. "Timeout. I can't recapture twenty years in one night. I can't do it. I just can't." Troy, realizing that he has caused Erica undue pressure and perhaps pushed too hard drilling her with his questions, apologizes. "Look I'm sorry. I guess I'm kind of anxious. Twenty years…that's a long time to all of a sudden just lose. I understand the strain this is putting on you, but this is my life, and I don't remember it."

Erica wraps her arms around Troy to comfort him. She kisses him on the cheek and comes around to kiss his lips, but this is a feeling so distant from him. For the second time, he turns away from her lips, kissing her on the cheek.

She reassures him that everything is going to be all right and turns the TV on remotely to divert his attention to something else. She flips from channel to channel and stops at the sound of a roaring crowd cheering during a basketball game. The cheering sends a shooting pain across his forehead and Troy covers his ears to try to drown out some of the noise and ease his pain.

Erica rushes over to Troy and asks, "What? What is it?"

"Ohhhh, the crowd. The noise. My head, it hurts."

Erica is concerned. "Remembering something?"

Troy holds his head in his hands. "No, just pain. But tell me, did I play sports?"

"Here we go, more questions. Yeah, you played basketball in college."

"Was I good?"

"The star player."

"What college?"

Erica, annoyed by his questioning, blows some steam and huffs. "Look, I'm tired. I'm done with this. It's been a long couple of weeks for both of us. I almost lost you and now…"

Troy, trapped in a memory of nothing and wanting so bad to remember all that he has lost, ruefully finishes her sentence. "I guess I'm being kind of insensitive. I'm being thoughtless. You've been through a lot, too. Forgive an old man for not thinking of you."

Troy kisses Erica on the forehead and pulls her into his arms, hugging her. Erica smiles and kisses him on the cheek, then moves to his lips, but this time before he can dismiss her feeble attempt at intimacy, she changes and turns her cheek to him.

And still, another change. He releases her and crosses back over to the sofa.

Feeling rejected, Erica moves to the bedroom door. "I-I'm going to bed. Coming?" Troy picks up the remote and starts flipping channels, ignoring her. "Did you hear me?"

"Later." Troy is trying to escape what he doesn't know about or feel for her. "I'm gonna hang out here with the television for a little bit. Good night."

Erica ponders his actions, then slides the double doors together. A couple of seconds pass, then the doors slide back open. Erica stands in the doorway.

"You know, I lost something, too."

Troy, puzzled and not sure he understands, asks, "What?"

"Twenty years. I lost twenty years with you."

Troy turns the television off. Reluctantly, he walks over to Erica. She backs up to the bed as he enters. He slides the doors closed.

Hours later, the double doors slide open, and Troy comes out, wrapped in a blanket to keep his naked body warm from the chill of the winter's night. He sits on the sofa and opens the photo album sitting on the table in front of him. He turns the pages studying the pictures. Concern, worry, and frustration shadow his face.

A flashback, he recalls the unemotional moments he had just spent with Erica.

No desire, no love, no emotion. She struggled to get pleasure from an unpleasurable moment. Troy lay in bed underneath her, motionless, while she tried very hard to seduce him with her love. After all, this was her first time with human flesh, and it was not quite the same after losing her virginity to a plastic sexual toy.

"You're not trying," she said.

Troy apologized. "I'm sorry. I can't create what's not there. I'm sorry."

Erica stopped her efforts at lovemaking and rolled over on her side, her back to him. He lay in bed staring into space, wondering about empty emotions that he's expected to feel, expected to perform, but just weren't there.

A tear slides down Erica's face.

Chapter 24

IT AIN'T A SOCIAL VISIT

THE PRO BASKETBALL locker room at Templeton Center is a real zoo of balls and male testosterone. It's the after game wrap-up. Some players are completely dressed and leave. Others kid around with one another while they finish dressing. One player sniffs in the air as if he smells something foul. He fans his nose to clear the air. The all-star, Philben comes out of the shower with a towel wrapped around his waist and one thrown over his shoulder.

As he passes by a player's opened locker, Philben cringes and slaps the locker door shut with the towel. He fans around the locker with the towel.

"Whew! What are you keeping in there—a dead rat—your mother?

"Watch it now. Leave my mother out of this."

"Man, we don't need you to go all psycho on us now."

Philben and some of the other players standing close by fan their noses. They all stare at the basketball player's locker wondering what the hell that foul smell could be that permeates the air. They jokingly harass him.

The basketball player defends himself. "Well, don't look at me."

Philben makes another wisecrack. "Man, cleanliness is next to godliness. You got something you wanna tell us?"

The player replies, "It's not me. I smelled it, too. I thought it was one of you."

SURROUNDED BY A slew of open photo albums, yearbooks, boxes, and old newspaper clippings scattered on the floor in the family room, Jill sat on the floor searching through a stack of the albums. She flips through album after album and page after page and turns to a newspaper clipping about how Troy led his college team to their second straight national college championship. Then she turns to a picture of Troy, Jamal, and several other players hugged together, posing with some cheerleaders. She stares at the women's faces and studies them, trying to see if one of them resembles her female attacker, but there is no similarity.

She turns to a college photo of young Troy and young Jill wrapped in each other's arms, kissing. Young Jamal's head peeks around them, looking up at them. The memory of them all together brings tears to her eyes. A tear drops on the photo.

The doorbell rings. Jill composes herself and wipes her face. Madi rushes down the stairs and peeks out through the side window to see who it is. She opens the door.

Jill calls out to Madi, "Honey, who is it?"

"Him."

"Who's him?"

Jill comes around the corner from the family room. Standing in the doorway is Detective Shameus. She responds a bit curt, her attitude tarnished by their first meeting. "Oh, you." Just as quickly as she dismisses him, she recognizes that he is there to help by the somewhat concerned tone in his voice.

"I have some news."

Jill, feeling hopeful, is on edge, waiting to hear. "Well?"

And Detective Shameus, back to his normal irritating mood, says, "Well, it ain't a social visit. But, we found something, and I need you to come with me."

———⊗⊗⊙———

THE WALLS, A shade of light gray, seem to close in on her as she walks down the long corridor with Detective Shameus. Jill feels a slight chill traveling up and down her arms. As they get closer to the entrance, she is able to read the words, "City Morgue" stamped on the glass door. She trembles with trepidation not knowing what to expect. The blood in her veins seems to throb up and down her arms. Is this an anxiety attack she's feeling? Jill hesitates to collect herself before entering. In her mind she thinks, *I don't want to know.*

Detective Shameus pats her on the arm, comforting her, and asks, "Are you going to be ok?"

Strange, there is a human side to this man whom Jill has framed as cynical, erratic, moody, and cold. They enter the dreary looking morgue.

The female coroner wearing protective goggles and a mask examines a woman's body, grayish in color with black and blue patches about her face. The coroner looks at her computer, examining the cadaver's inner body parts. Then she uses an oscillating saw to make a lateral cut down the chest area.

Detective Shameus nods at the coroner, and she stops to open a morgue drawer. The detective pulls back the sheet to reveal a very decomposed body. The dark-brown skin is sunken in and gaunt in some places on the frame of the body. Pieces of pink flesh peek out from under the ash brown skin that has peeled away a little around his face.

A compassionate Detective Shameus asks, "I know this may be hard, Mrs. Norton, but can you identify him?" Water wells in Jill's shocked eyes forming tears that trickle down her face. She nods her head. "Jamal. It's Jamal."

Detective Shameus beckons to the coroner. She moves over to another morgue drawer and pulls it open.

Detective Shameus asks, "And him?"

Jill almost drops to the floor. Her stomach clamps from weakness at the sight when the pale-grayish skin exposes someone else that she knows and loves.

Detective Shameus wraps his arms around her to break her fall. "You gonna be all right?"

A mix of emotions—sadness and hope—fills Jill's heart. She breathes a sigh of relief and closes her eyes for a second of solemn gratitude that it's not Troy. But the sadness of knowing her long-time neighbor and friend is gone overcomes her. She sobs mightily in Detective Shameus's arms.

He comforts her, stroking and patting her on the back, a bit awkward for it is not his normal temperament.

He whispers, "You know him?"

"Yes, that's Ron. The three of them went to the all-star pro basketball game together in Las Vegas."

"That explains why they were found stuffed in a wall behind the lockers," he comments.

"What?"

"Yes, I'm sorry, but that's where they found them."

"Oh my God, murdered? How did they get here?" Then she snaps her fingers. "Ohhhh...the chain Ron wore around his neck with his medical identification info."

Detective Shameus confirms that. "The chain provided us with enough information to trace Ron back to your husband, and you just confirmed it."

She asks, "Was there anyone else?"

"No."

"So my husband may still be alive. The impostor did this."

Detective Shameus pulls out his cigarette case and begins tapping an e-cigarette on it. "Going down that road again?"

She becomes irritated. "Why aren't you out looking for him?"

"Oh, trust me, we will be. Three people are dead, and your husband has connections with all of them."

Jill baffled, repeats, "Three?"

"Yeah, we found the body of a kid, a nineteen-year-old teenager. I just got some paperwork today from that investigation. Your daughter had been hanging out with this kid."

"Rance?"

"Yes."

"How do I tell her?"

Although saddened by the loss of their dear friends and the young man, Jill feels a sense of relief that perhaps Troy is still alive and finally maybe the detective knows the truth. "So you believe me now."

"I believe there's a connection, and this might explain his abrupt disappearance. We need him for questioning, and I figure you know more than you're telling us."

Why? She wonders. None of this makes sense to her. *What is the woman and the Troy impersonator's involvement in all of this?* But now the detective might be looking at her husband as a suspect.

"My husband had nothing to do with this. They were his friends. What can I say to make you believe that he had nothing to do with this?"

Detective Shameus retorts, "I've got two dead bodies that I'm investigating plus a third one now, and your husband's missing. No, you say your husband has been kidnapped. How convenient. Your husband had connections with all three. Tell me, what should I think?"

Chapter 25

CREEPY

TROY, CURLED UP on the sofa, snores in his sleep. A loud scream from fear awakens him, and he jumps up out of his sleep. Staring at him from the TV is a woman screaming at the top of her lungs as if death stalks her. *Now that's creepy,* he thinks to himself. He lies back down and starts watching the creepy show.

Minutes later, he thinks he hears a noise coming from the bedroom door, which captures his attention, but the door is shut. Thinking that what he hears are just sounds of the house and perhaps he's hearing things, Troy relaxes and continues watching the creep show on television.

But, someone is watching him and following his every move.

Then, Troy thinks he hears a footstep across the room in the dark recesses of the hallway leading to the kitchen. Eerie. He calls out, "Erica?" But, there is no response.

He gets up and walks over to the bedroom double doors and quietly slides them open a little, just enough to confirm that Erica is in bed. She sleeps soundly. He returns to the sofa and blows it off, thinking that *he must be a bit on edge.* He has endured a lot over the past weeks. To add to his anxiety and frustrations, now his head feels like a hammer is pounding against it. He squints from the pain and strokes his forehead sweeping across it back and forth trying to calm his nerves and relax. He returns to watching the television to ease the tension and allay his concerns. Troy relaxes back down on the sofa flipping the channels and is drawn to a basketball game. The sounds he thought he was hearing seem to have gone away.

⸺∞⸺

THE DOOR TO Madi's bedroom is slightly cracked. She works away on her laptop, restructuring some of the yearbook women's faces to represent how they might look present day. The house is quiet, but Madi hears the stairs creak. She looks in the direction of the partially opened door and calls out, "Is someone there?"

Dead silence.

Madi chuckles. "I must be hearing things." She returns to keying on her laptop.

A few seconds pass, and she hears the steps creak again.

She calls out, "Mom?" But again, there is no response. Slow but steady footsteps come up the stairs. Madi's heart rate elevates and begins to pound fiercely in her chest as she listens to the steps come closer and closer. Could it be that the kidnappers have come back? Will it be worse this time? As the steps come closer to her door, she grabs a heavy book from a bookshelf and stands behind the door, waiting for her attacker.

The door creaks as a hand eases the door open. Her heart pounds faster racing with fear. Madi raises the book high to pound her attacker over the head but quickly recognizes her mother. With a sigh of relief, she clutches the book to her heart.

"Mom! I thought you were a burglar—or worse, those people had come back."

Jill hugs Madi. "I'm sorry, darling."

"Why didn't you answer me?"

"My mind was totally consumed by something disturbing. I guess I didn't hear you."

She's sad and anguish covers her face as she guides Madi over to the bed.

"Honey, sit down." They sit down on the edge of the bed.

She pats Madi's hands and cups them between hers. The look on Jill's face raises concern in Madi.

"Mom, what's wrong?"

Her motherly love does not want to break the shattering news to Madi. She responds, "I don't know how to tell you."

"Daddy? Is he all right?"

"I believe he is."

"What are you saying?"

"It's your Uncle—"

"—Ron? What, what happened to him?"

"He's gone, honey…"

Madi is horrified by this disturbing news and can't believe what she's hearing.

Jill tells her even more. "Jamal, too." Jill graphically describes how the police found their badly decomposed bodies in the locker room walls at the Templeton Center.

Madi is devastated. "Murdered?"

"Yes."

Madi can't believe what her mother has just told her. It seemed that it was just yesterday that she had just seen her Uncle Ron. A tear drops.

"There's more," her mother says.

"No, no, not Dad."

"Rance, your friend, Rance. The police have his body, too."

"What?"

"And...the police think your father had something to do with his death."

"No, that's not possible. Dad didn't kill anyone."

"I know. You don't have to convince me."

Madi is puzzled by all of this. "Do you think this has something to do with Daddy disappearing?"

Jill replies, "I know it does. Remember, the past weeks..."

"No, months..."

"...we lived with an imposter—"

"—metal monster," Madi interrupts.

She returns to the computer, even more determined to find the missing pieces in this puzzle. "Who *is* this woman?" she asks.

Jill adds, "And what has she created?"

Night crawls and Madi sits at her computer continuing her facial reconstruction of one of the cheerleaders. Using the age-progression software from her class, she divides the face into four sections, then modifies each section to show age progression, manipulating the eyes, cheeks, chin, and then the hair. She creates a composite of one of the women and performs this process for several of the other women's pictures. Meanwhile, Jill sits on the floor going through the yearbook.

Madi pulls up several of the completed reconstructed pictures on the monitor. "Mom, take a look at these." Jill looks over Madi's shoulder at the pictures. "What do you think?"

Jill studies the first one. "No."

Madi pulls up another picture. Jill ponders it before saying, "No resemblance. None." Madi pulls up another one. Jill shakes her head, and again, she says, "No." Madi goes through several more.

There's something about the last picture that catches Jill's eye. "Wait. Go back."

Madi goes back to a picture that resembles Erica. "This one?"

Jill stares at the picture and notices the small scar on the woman's cheek, then touches her finger to the scar on the screen, studying it. She has a flashback of the woman who attacked her.

Madi asks, "Is this her? I was just playing around with it, trying to improve her."

Jill has reservations and some uncertainty. "It looks like her. The scar, I don't remember it. I'm just not sure."

Madi, hopeful, says, "It…it's a start. And to think I almost did not include her, 'cause she clearly was not Daddy's type."

But Jill still has lingering doubts. She shakes her head. "I just don't know, baby. I just don't know."

"Mom, I have an idea," Madi says. "Why don't we post the pictures around town and ask if anyone recognizes them? Maybe even check with the police."

"Maybe," Jill remarks. Saddened by it all, she adds, "I just hope nothing has happened to your fath—"

But before Jill can finish her words, Madi interrupts her. "Nothing has, Mom."

In a show of solidarity and support, Jill hugs Madi, who begins to cry. Tears roll down Jill's face too, and Madi embraces her mother, reassuring her.

"I love you, Mom. He's all right. I know it. I know he is."

Jill and Madi hold each other tight, giving strength and comfort to each other.

Chapter 26

A Different Family

Troy stands at the mirror combing his hair. He stops to run his fingers across a scar on his right shoulder. Erica walks up behind him and hugs him. She intertwines her fingers with his and rubs the scar with him. She watches their motions through the mirror.

Erica whispers in his ear, "Sensual. I could get turned on doing this."

"How did I get this?"

Erica shrugs her shoulders. "I don't know. It's just an old relic from the past."

Troy notices the scar on Erica's cheek. "You have one too."

"What?"

"A scar, you have one, too."

Erica immediately covers the scar with her hand, trying to hide her embarrassment.

He reassures her that the scar is nothing and kisses it on her cheek. "It doesn't change you."

Erica, longing for him to initiate some affection, puckers her lips and closes her eyes, leaning in toward

Troy for a deeper show of affection, their lips locking. Still, Troy is not there yet and dismisses the intimate emotional moment. Instead, he lays an apathetic kiss on her forehead.

His actions frustrate Erica. She becomes annoyed and throws a temper tantrum to express her discontent with his unemotional behavior. After all, in her mind, she is his wife. "I deserve your love, your touch, more than just these little childish pecks of adoration," she scolds.

Troy ignores her longing desire for him. He turns back to the mirror and continues to brush his hair. Erica's dark eyes penetrate through Troy, but she calms down and kisses the back of his shoulder. How much longer can she take his dismissals of affection? How much longer can she control him trying to convince him that theirs has been a love forever.

Later, Troy sits on the couch, bored and restless. He flips through magazine after magazine. A scuttling sound from the aquarium catches his ear. He throws the magazine down, crosses over to the aquarium, and starts tapping on the side of it. Curiosity piques his interest prompting him to investigate the sounds from inside the caves. "Must be something really creepy in here," he says.

The mix of gravel and sand covering the aquarium floor projects a coarse sound traveling up and down inside the caves. He leans up next to the side of the aquarium. "Come out, come out, whatever you are."

A hand brushes the back of Troy's neck, startles him. He jumps in his skin and the hairs on the back of his neck stand up.

Erica admonishes him, "Be careful. There may be something scary in there." Erica grabs her purse sitting on a chair.

"And where is my wife off to?" Troy asks.

"Wife, I love the sound of that." Erica sneaks a kiss and pecks Troy on the lips. "I am your wife, aren't I?"

Troy fakes a smile and goes back to tapping the sides of the aquarium. He hears the scratchy coarse sound again.

"Tell me what's inside?" he asks.

"Pets."

"Pets?"

Erica walks up to the aquarium and taps the side of the glass. Troy begins to toy with the invisible predators.

"Come out, babies, come out," he says. He taps on the glass.

"I wouldn't do that if I were you," Erica warns.

"Why, is something gonna grab me?" He laughs.

Erica explains her family dynamics and gives Troy a bit of history.

"Before you came along, they were my family."

"Your family?" Troy asks.

"A different kind of family. They were the closest thing to what I called, family. You see I never knew my mother. She died giving me life. My relationship with my father was a bit estranged. He blamed me for her death."

"But childbirth wasn't your fault."

"It doesn't matter. He blamed me and didn't love or want me, so these creatures became my family."

Troy, a bit stunned to hear what she developed an emotional bond with, jokingly says, "Creatures? Your family? Ok. Let's take a look at this family."

The white translucent pincers creep up to the cave entrance unnoticed by Troy. He playfully dangles his hands in the aquarium.

Erica distracts Troy by overpowering him with a kiss. He pulls his hand out of the aquarium and finally succumbs to her emotional need, wrapping his arms around her. This time he tries to feel but his kiss is still unfeeling and unemotional; he puts no effort in the kiss and abruptly stops.

His lack of affection, emotion, and acceptance toward her is insulting. "It's aggravating the way you treat me," she complains. "I deserve better."

Troy dismisses her mini tantrum and turns back to the aquarium rather annoyed. He does not understand why she does not understand his impassive behavior since he has no recollection of her. He presses his face against the side to get a closer look.

Erica jests, "Wanna see what's inside?" She guides Troy's hand back into the aquarium.

"Ooh, should I be scared?"

An albino scorpion lunges and spears the glass wall, missing Troy's hand by a hair but leaving a spray of milky secretion that trickles down the wall of the aquarium. Before retreating to its nocturnal domicile in the caves, the angry predator strikes through the gravel mixture as if it were looking for his prey. Blind like so many albino arthropods, its beady pink eyes can only sense a prey through sound.

Troy quickly jumps back, pulling his hand out. "Scorpions!" he yells. "What's the matter with you? Are you crazy?" He pushes Erica away, which aggravates her even more.

She explodes. "You called me crazy. I'm not!" Just as quickly as she insists that her psychological state is not abnormal, she flips the switch and apologizes, professing her love for him. "I didn't mean it. I love you."

But he is not dissuaded by her comments. "If this is love, then I don't want to see what hate looks like." Troy storms off.

Erica runs after him, pleading for his forgiveness. She attempts to kiss him, but he pushes her away. She calls to him as he moves closer to their bedroom. "I would never hurt you."

In his short memory of their relationship, it has been a rollercoaster of unbalanced emotional behavior. Erica cries and tries to explain her actions. "Although hurt has been with me all my life, I would never hurt you. I love you so much. And you love me, don't you?"

But he doesn't answer. He can't say what he doesn't feel, which Erica senses. She speaks quietly.

"You know how the male scorpion seduces his mate? He dances with her until he finds the right place to mate."

Troy, eager to understand this relationship with his alleged wife, responds, "Is that how we met?"

Erica continues, "It's called the promenade a deux, the dance of love."

"So we met at a dance?"

"He dances with her and makes love to her…" Her voice hardens. "Then she kills him."

Troy's eyes penetrate hers as if he could cut right through her with a knife stained with hate "Is that a threat?" He turns away and stomps into the bedroom even more vigilant.

"A warning, just a warning." She grabs him by the shoulder and again tries to explain that she would never hurt him. "Don't ever cross me," she says and then flips the switch on her disturbing personality behavior. She expresses her sorrow and wraps her arms around him from behind.

"I make you happy, don't I?"

Troy peels Erica's arms from around his waist.

"I have no memory of my past. I have lost the twenty years when we were supposed to love each other and that I don't understand—" He cuts his words off before he says anything else to hurt her or raise more questions in his mind about her.

Erica crosses over to a wooden dining chair, and she starts clawing and grinding her nails into it. At the same time, she begs to hear the words, "Tell me that you love me. That we belong together and always will."

Speechless, Troy doesn't know what to say or how to respond to her sickening mania. It is beyond comprehension. His eyes focus on the wood shavings falling into the seat of the chair as Erica continues to grind and scrape her nails into the wood.

"You love me?"

Erica grinds her short and chipped nails deeper into the wood, down to her fingertips, but they have become numb from the many times this act has been performed.

Troy tries to get her to stop. "Erica!"

But she doesn't feel or see the blood seeping from her broken skin at the fingertips. "You love me?"

He grabs her fingers, bringing them to her face so she can see her fingertips hoping this would impact her to stop.

She eyes the blood and cries, "Promise me you'll never leave me."

Troy, in empathetic bewilderment, hugs her to comfort her.

She pleads, "Promise me."

He hesitates and doesn't say the words. Again, he lays an apathetic kiss on her forehead.

A few minutes later, he gently rubs the blood away from her fingertips under running water in the bathroom sink. She's squeamish, and flinches and whimpers. "Ouch. Ouch!"

Troy reprimands her about getting so upset to the degree that she hurts herself, but she doesn't hear a word he says. Her only concern is hearing him say the words she so eagerly yearns for.

"But you do love me?"

He hesitates, wrestling with the thought and so much ambiguity. He does not understand what he could ever have wanted in this woman, what he could ever have seen in this woman to marry her. He responds, "We're married, and I love the woman I married."

Hearing those words, in Erica's imaginary and crazed mind, she is convinced that he loves her and has completely given himself to her. She smiles.

Chapter 27

I Love The Woman I Married

Iт's а busy street in the downtown shopping area of this Georgia suburban town, Tarleton. People are walking up and down the cobbled streets and sidewalks shopping in a mixture of Victorian and Antebellum-styled old town storefronts and eateries. Some carry shopping bags labeled with the specialty boutique stores that line the streets. Others stroll down the sidewalk going from shop to shop.

The Norton's red convertible sports car races up to the curb and parks. Jill hops out of the passenger side with a stack of posters cradled in her arms. She takes a deep breath.

"I don't know which is worse—your dad's MLC or your teenage raging hormones."

"But you got here in one piece," Madi murmurs in an undertone as she hops out of the car.

"Thank God there's a God," Jill says.

Madi comes around to Jill, and they discuss the plan of action to distribute the posters of the eight aged-progressed women's pictures. The poster reads, "HAVE YOU

Seen Me? Contact 1-800-FIND_ME." The plan—each would take a side of the street and post the pictures in addition to checking with store owners and passersby,

One final check before they separate. "Cell phone?" Jill asks.

"Check." Madi confirms, pulling it out to show her.

"Thirty minutes. Meet back here in thirty minutes, Madi." Jill kisses Madi on the forehead and hugs her. Then Madi runs across the street.

Jill walks down the street posting pictures on sign-posts. She also stops a few people on the street to show them the posters, but they all shake their heads. None of them recognize any of the pictures.

Meanwhile, Madi enters a consignment boutique that carries upscale women's clothes of the vintage kind. She has a stack of posters in her arms and walks up to the counter. A middle-aged hippie woman straight out of the 70s wearing a long ankle-length colorful skirt and psychedelic scarf wrapped around her head comes out to the counter from a back area. She's somewhat quirky and greets Madi with a peace sign. "Peace." There's a mysterious aura that emanates from her as she walks up closer into Madi's space.

Their eyes meet and she stares into Madi's eyes, making her feel a little awkward and uncomfortable so much that Madi looks away for a second, then back at the woman. The woman says, "I can see it in your eyes. He's all right, but lost."

Madi frowns. She doesn't know what to make of this woman and wonders if she is some loon or blessed with spiritual gifts. "What—what did you say?

The mystic woman responds again. "He's all right."

"You see my father? Are you clairvoyant or something? Where is he?"

Overwhelmed by her multiple questions, the mystic woman gestures a hand brake to slow Madi down with her quizzing. "Stop. I can't tell you something I don't know."

"But you said my father."

"No, that's not what I said."

"But you knew he was lost."

"I said he's all right, a man. Is your father missing?"

"Yes."

Madi, somewhat baffled, says, "Well, maybe you can help me with this, also. I'm looking for the owner or the manager."

"That would be me," she says.

Madi shows the posters to the woman and asks if it would be alright to place them in the store's window. The woman nods her head, yes. Madi thanks her and turns to exit but bumps into Jasmine before leaving the store. And just a few months back, she had approached Troy with the surveys questionnaire at the recreation center. Jasmine and Madi exchange hellos. She inquires about her "good-looking dad ." Suspicious, Madi is reluctant to respond, unsure of Jasmine's trustworthiness, and tells her that he's all right.

Inquisitive, Jasmine says, "What are those?"

Madi shows her a poster. "I'm trying to find out if anyone has seen or recognizes any of these women."

"You know them?" Jasmine asks.

"It's a school project."

Jasmine looks over the photos and raises an eyebrow. "She's missing? Funny, she's missing. I know her."

"You know her?" Madi anxiously asks.

"I don't 'know her, know her. We—I mean the company I work for—did some marketing work for her... Pendergrass Sanitarium." Jasmine explains that the woman is a psychiatrist, and Troy filled out one of the woman's surveys for the marketing company.

With hope in her eyes, Madi skirts toward the door. As she passes the mystic woman, she thanks her. The woman replies, "Hope says, don't give up on your dad."

"He's alive, isn't he?" Madi smiles. The mystery woman smiles back and throws another peace sign back at Madi as she leaves the store. She pulls her cell phone out. "Mom, good news. Meet me at the car."

Madi meets her mom, very excited. She tells her about the clairvoyant woman and what she learned from Jasmine.

Jill eagerly responds, "Ok, let's go hunting and find hope."

Chapter 28

FINDING HOPE

ERICA SITS IN the driver's seat of the Jeep Rover with the motor running. Troy stands at the open driver's door feeling restless, wanting to escape the prison ward that seems to have a hold on him and not knowing who and where he is, he's trapped. He wants to put the puzzle together, fill in the holes, and solve the missing twenty years of his life.

"When do I get to come into town to see our other pets, those exotic ones?"

"Soon."

"And when is soon?"

"When the doctor releases you. You'll see him next week."

Troy shuts the door and leans through the car window. He kisses Erica on her cheek.

This short-lived moment of affection excites her. She so desperately longs for this that she quickly hops out of the car and rushes to him. She kisses him back with such force that her lips press painfully against his. He pries himself away from this absurdity.

Erica pitifully asks, "You do love me, don't you? You kissed me."

He can't answer with an emotion he doesn't feel. So, he backs away from the car. "You should go now."

Erica sadly returns to the driver's seat heavy-hearted feeling the rejection. As Troy waves goodbye, her sadness turns into anger. She quickly speeds off in the car. Troy ponders her actions.

⸻ ◦◦◦ ⸻

TENSION AND ANXIETY riddle through Jill as she sits on an airplane destined for answers and finding Troy. A flight attendant stops to give her a drink.

"This should relax you," she says. "Your tequila, with a twist of hope."

⸻ ◦◦◦ ⸻

MOMENTS AFTER ERICA is away from the house, Troy hunts through the bedroom drawers on a mission, searching with urgency. He finds a picture of Erica and him embracing on a sailboat. Whatever, they may have between them just seems so unreal to him. He ponders on the thought. Was he really happy with her? How did they meet? Answers are what he needs. Answers are what he will find.

He rushes to the study hunting through drawer after drawer, tossing and pushing things aside. He thumbs through several books on the shelf and finds a photo album hiding behind two books. Flipping through the pages, he finds a cutout picture of young Erica with the bird's nest hairdo. "Weird," he says.

Then he flips to another page in the photo album. A magazine article with a picture of Erica and the caption underneath reads, "DR. ERICA PENDERGRASS."

"A doctor?" Troy slaps the book shut.

He opens a netbook sitting on the desk. "Now, who is this crazy woman?" He Googles "DR. ERICA PENDERGRASS."

A pop-up news report flashes on the screen that shows a picture of Ron and Jamal and the headline, TWO MEN FOUND DEAD STUFFED IN TEMPLETON CENTER LOCKER-ROOM WALL. Troy stares at the popup and then has a flashback to a pool of blood. It clouds his mind, but it doesn't mean anything. He can't make the connection and dismisses this blur of the past.

He returns to Erica's picture on the screen and clicks on it. It hyperlinks to an article about Dr. Erica Pendergrass, computer neuroscientist and psychiatrist, breaking ground at Pendergrass Sanitarium. Troy gets on the phone and calls the number listed under the picture. The phone clicks and disconnects.

"What...? Hello, hello."

Troy eyes a shadowy reflection in the mirror hanging on the wall, which startles him. Slowly, he puts the phone down and turns around to gaze upon a shocking sight, his double standing across the room.

"So we meet again."

"Again?" Troy asks, somewhat disoriented.

"Handsome, aren't we?"

"I don't understand. Are you my brother?"

"Closer."

The synthetic replica explains that Troy has found the pieces of the puzzle and how he's starting to fill in the gaps.

"You've discovered that she's a scientist."

"Yes."

"And she deals with the mind."

"Yes."

"And your curiosity?" The lookalike's shadow comes closer up to Troy.

Troy remarks, "Is fatal."

The double confirms his dim plight. "Something like that."

"So the plan is kill me, and you take my place?"

"No. Something better."

"But why? She isn't my wife, is she?"

"No, but something tipped you off, right."

Troy buys time trying to understand and get more answers. At the same time, he wants to figure out an escape. Slyly, he looks around the room for something to use as a weapon. "She's strange. Her sudden outbursts of anger. The constant need to be reassured that I love her. She's a psycho bitch. So, where do you—"

"—fit in? My role, along with convincing your family that I was you, was to also make sure you could never go back home."

"I have a family and can never go back home. What do you mean?"

The double explains how the article he just skimmed over relates to Troy. He details how those dead men were his friends, and how they all went on a weekend trip that turned deadly for them, but started a new life for Troy.

"New life? But what about Erica—her life, her practice?"

The double further explains how she gave that up too, and found this secluded out-of-the-way village thousands of miles away from both of their previous lives.

"And except for the occasional seasonal skiing, no one comes here. No one knows you're here—only that you own an exotic pet shop."

Seeing this façade of him and hearing the details of this story with new information shoots a pain through Troy's head. He grimaces.

"Remembering something?" the double asks.

"I don't understand any of this. This is preposterous, unbelievably insane."

"And it only gets better," the lookalike continues. "Those two men, those two friends of yours were found dead in a locker room."

"I don't remember them."

His double responds, "Unfortunately for you, that doesn't matter. The police think you murdered them and a third one, too, 'cause you did. No, I mean your lookalike—me—I did it. And now you are a wanted man, a wanted man who can't go home."

JILL ARRIVES AT her destination to Tremblant, a small quaint town somewhat popular as a ski town. It's the end of the ski season, but the streets are busier than normal with still a few tourists there. She walks down the sidewalk past several boutiques and restaurants, talking to Madi on the cell phone. She lets her know that she has arrived and compliments her. "You did good work. You got me here, sweetheart."

Suddenly, a ray of hope, she spots a man walking ahead of her whose build, hair color, and wavy locks resemble Troy's. "Madi, I'll call you back." Jill follows the man who enters a flower shop. She inconspicuously peeks in through the flower shop window watching him. Madi and she have become a real Sherlock Holmes and Watson team.

The man purchases a lovely array of multicolored blossoms. He collects the arrangement in his arms and exits the flower shop. As he leaves, a passerby crosses in front of Jill preventing her from getting a better look at his face. She calls out, "Troy!" But, he continues walking and never responds. That moment of hope quickly fades to bewilderment and confusion. She follows him down the sidewalk and again they are separated by a group of ski tourists coming out of a restaurant who gets in between them. However, she's able to see him ahead of them and follows.

At last he stops, and to her surprise, he walks up to a sleekly beautiful woman leaning against a car. He kisses her and then presents her with the beautiful bouquet. Now Jill gets a better look at him, and sadly disappointed, sees it's not Troy. Hope quickly disappears.

She continues her vigilant pursuit down the sidewalk of Tremblant. The storybook colorful rooftops are like a fairy tale village. And a storybook fairy tale is what Jill is hoping for, a happy ending finding her love, Troy.

She approaches the window of an exotic pet shop and looks in. A kinkajou paws through a cage at the window which catches Jill's eye. Jill places her hand up against the shop window, matching the kinkajou's paw. "Cute," she says. The kinkajou's eyes have a warm look about them as if they were smiling, which brings some comfort to Jill at a time when there is so much sadness and frustration.

Inside, Erica waits on a female customer, an elderly teacher, who looks at some rare bugs.

"These will be great for my biology students."

Jill peeks inside the shop window, watching Erica wait on the teacher. She thinks she recognizes her. Quickly, she pulls out a folded poster from inside her purse and looks at both, the poster and the woman in the shop. "It's her," she mumbles. She darts away from the window, bittersweet—frightened and at the same time excited with hope that maybe she has found Troy and alive.

Jill peeks back in the window and as Erica shows the teacher some bugs, she is momentarily interrupted. She gets a quick glimpse of Jill staring at her through the window. Quickly, Jill darts off, to keep from being seen and alarm Erica.

The teacher asks, "Can you deliver?"

Erica, consumed with worry, nervously answers, "Wh-what was that?"

"Deliver? Can you deliver?"

Erica thinking that she saw Jill ignores the teacher and does not answer. Panicking, she rushes the teacher to finish her shopping. "Is that it?"

She stops to look at some other insects. "Did you hear me?" The teacher asks, a bit annoyed with Erica's sudden impatience.

Erica, preoccupied looking back at the window and distracted by whom she thinks she sees says, "What?"

The teacher asks again, "Do you deliver?"

Erica cuts her short. "Look, we're closing early today."

"But I'm...I'm still looking."

"Not anymore." Erica quickly ushers the teacher out the door.

The teacher becomes furious and yells at Erica. "What? Why I never—" The teacher storms off down the sidewalk.

Erica looks both ways for Jill, who has disappeared. She quickly flips the OPEN sign on the door to CLOSED and whips her cell phone out. Frustrated, she calls her synthetic creation. While talking to him, she grinds her nails into a wooden chair. Traces of her frustration and psychotic behavior are already present in the deep lines of scratch marks embedded in the chair.

"She's here."

"I know," comes the answer from the other party on the phone.

"Where is she staying?"

"The Inn," says the double.

Erica grinds deeper into the wooden chair. Blood drips down the side of the chair from the tips of her fingers. She screams at the phone, cursing him for not taking care of Jill the first time, because this is a problem that should have been eradicated.

But he reminds her that she has a family.

"Well, then, after you get rid of her, get rid of the family!"

———

DEEP IN A secluded wooded area at The Inn sits a very rustic and warm-looking log cabin. The lights hanging among the tall pine trees shine down on several cabins spaced far enough apart to give guests quiet peace and privacy, something Jill needs to relax her unnerved spirits worrying about Troy. She adds more logs to the fireplace and rustles them with the poker to build a bigger fire. Then she holds her hands in front of the fireplace to warm them.

After warming up, she begins to unpack her clothes and pulls a family picture of Troy, Madi, and her from the luggage. She traces the outline of Troy and Madi's form with her fingers. Then out of nowhere, in the quiet night, Jill thinks she hears a faint whisper.

"Jill."

She looks around for the sound and crosses over to the window. She looks out to see nothing. Is the sound her imagination, her nerves or is someone really there?

Jill finishes unpacking and starts her shower. Again, feeling like she's not alone; someone is watching. She looks out the window again to see nothing but the pitch blackness of the still night shadowing across the glowing white snow. "I've gotta get a grip," she fusses to herself. She relaxes and overcomes her anxieties as she stands under the warm shower water flowing down her back. The beads of water sprinkling on her face calm her.

Outside, the presence Jill sensed watching her is lurking around and watching from the woods. His robotic X-ray eyes penetrate the log cabin walls and find a naked Jill finishing up her shower. It takes him back to a virtual flashback of her getting out of the shower at home when he gave her the necklace for a wedding anniversary gift. He'd kissed the nape of her neck, then embraced her and passionately kissed her lips.

He walks through the mushy snow up to the log cabin window and peers in, watching her climb into bed. She grabs the picture, pressing it close to her heart. Tears roll down her cheeks.

Hours pass. Jill, curled up in bed and still hugging the picture in her arms, sleeps deeply, undisturbed from the eerie sounds of the late night. An owl hoots and wolves howl in the distance. Then a hand slowly brushes over her neck. The lookalike stands over her, looking down watching her sleep with his white eyes. She stirs but does not awaken and turns away from him. A bottle of sleeping pills sits on the nightstand next to her bed.

He has another fleeting virtual memory racing through his mind—when he sensuously danced the tango with Jill. His hand had traveled up and down her curvaceous body, and he asked her, "So you dance?"

"Only with my lover," she responds.

The door shuts and Jill awakens. She follows the sound that she thinks came from the door to only see darkness. Thinking that her imagination is running wild again, she grabs the family picture that has slid down and lies next to her. She hugs it close into her bosom for comfort. The imposter has gone.

Next morning, Jill drives down a narrow two-lane road, glancing over at a map sitting on the passenger's seat. Her eyes focus on a circled spot on the map that reads, "Farbinger Farms." It is the affluent subdivision where the ski resort homes sit on several acres. Miles of wooded terrain separate the homes from each other. One could drive a few miles before seeing the next house.

Driving farther down the road, she passes a sign with an arrow pointing west to Farbinger Farms that reads one mile on the left. Fearing the worst, she pulls over to the side of the road and stops briefly to pull out a gun from the glove compartment. She removes the safety and stuffs it in her purse.

NOW TROY IS in the study leafing through the pages of several books trying to find something interesting to read. He skims over the pages of the different books and finds one. He tucks the book under his arm and exits the room.

Jill leaves her car a little distance away from the house where Madi's investigation has led her to and walks up to a window. She peeps into the study but sees no one. Then, Troy enters with the book and a coffee cup. Maybe, Madi's efforts have paid off. Her heart flutters hoping that finally she has found her love. But then a darkness of uncertainty takes over. She looks at his hand to see if it is bandaged. No bandage, confirmation of what is real and what is not.

Finally, the search is over. She believes it is Troy. He walks out of the room and she tries to follow by moving to another window around the house, but this time, he is nowhere in sight.

"Looking for something?" Troy startles Jill from behind.

She turns around and smiles.

"Can I help you?" he asks.

"I kind of got—"

"—lost?" he asks.

"Yeah." Jill's eyes water when she sees him. She wonders why he does not recognize her. Nervous and at the same time elated to see the man she loves—the man she did not know was dead or alive, she tries to come up with an excuse and stutters.

"My-my-my car, it…stopped.

"Where?"

"Down the road."

Troy pats Jill on the shoulder to console her. "Everything is going to be all right. I can help you."

"You're nice to help a stranger."

"I'd help any damsel in distress."

Of course he would. Troy has always been a kind and considerate man.

"Thank you," she says. "I don't know what I would have done if I hadn't stumbled upon your place." Troy pulls out the car keys from inside his coat pocket. They get in the car and drive down the narrow two lane road. Jill thinks to herself, *hope is alive.*

Chapter 29

TRUTH HURTS

AS THEY DRIVE down the road, Troy questions Jill wondering how she ended up at Farbinger Farms, considering that the area is not on a main road and kind of out of the way from the nearest town.

"Farbinger Farms is not on the main road, so what were you doing out here?"

"Like I said, I got kind of turned around, lost. Then the car just stopped."

He allays her anxiety by saying, "No worries. It's a good thing you came upon our house."

Jill questions him carefully trying to find out what happened and figure out why he does not recognize her. She probes even more inquiring to find out how he found such a remote location from the town.

"I can't explain anything," Troy admits. "The truth is, I don't remember. I apologize for my memory loss. My wife says I have amnesia from head injuries that I suffered in a car accident."

"Wife? Amnesia?" Her heart collapses hearing him refer to someone else as his wife and not having any memory of her. She wants to reveal the truth but perhaps it is too soon. She is very cautious not to arouse any suspicions about her and calmly tries to conceal her emotional disappointment. "So you don't remember anything?"

"No. It's like my past—twenty years of my life just didn't exist."

It is disturbing to hear the man she loves and knows as her husband refer to another woman as his wife. She looks away out the window to keep Troy from seeing her tears. It's almost unbearable, the pain of knowing that her husband, only inches away, does not recognize her and has no memory of her.

But she composes herself and ponders. Is the woman pretending to be his wife the same woman who kidnapped him because it looked like her at the pet shop? What about the eerie robot that impersonated him? Where is he? Will he attack again?

"Your wife? What's her name?"

"Erica. Erica Miller. And your name?" he asks.

"It's Jill. Jill Norton."

She longs for Troy to remember her, desires his touch, and wants him to take her in his arms and end this horrible nightmare, so she continues interrogating him.

"Does the name Norton mean anything to you?"

"No. Should it?"

"No," she reluctantly replied. Then she says, "You know my name, but I don't know yours."

"It's Troy."

A Calvern Caves sign points to the right. They follow the directions on the sign and turn right. Troy reconfirms, "Calvern Caves…Huh."

Jill's car is parked in front of the opening to the caves. Troy pulls up and parks alongside it.

"You're awfully brave."

"Why do you say that?" Jill asks.

"You did come here by yourself."

"Yes."

"And you don't know anyone here?"

"Well, that's not quite true."

"What do you mean?" Troy ask with a puzzled look.

"There's something you should know." She takes a deep breath not knowing what to expect or how he will react. "It was no accident that the car just happened to break down."

"What are you saying?"

"I can help you rediscover your history.

He doesn't understand and asks, "Do I know you?"

"You have a family. You…you have a daughter."

"A daughter. That's not possible. You're mistaken. My wife told me there are no children."

Then Jill's eyes water. She pulls a wallet-size photo from her jacket pocket. "She lied to you, Troy. See, this is Madi, your daughter." Jill shows him the picture.

Troy takes the picture and studies it.

"I have a daughter…"

"She's a good kid. She misses you so."

"How old?"

"Sixteen."

"I have a sixteen-year-old."

"She's smart, too. She's the reason I was able to find you."

"Really."

"She's a computer whiz kid and plays basketball. You taught her."

He looks at her. "My wife said I was a college star."

Hearing Troy refer to Erica as his wife infuriates Jill, and she simply cannot control her anger. "She's not your wife."

Troy seems confused and disillusioned by her behavior. "Don't get upset. I don't know you. You could be lying."

"No, she attacked me and abducted you."

"You're lying. This is not true." He finds it all so hard to believe.

Jill explains how Madi is learning forensic science artistry in school and used his college yearbook to restructure several photos of women from then to the present day. "We had a hunch. Madi reconfigured several women from college with an age-progression software."

"Smart."

"Yes, she is."

"And, we got lucky." She then explains how Madi and she posted the photos around their hometown.

He interrupts. "Home, where is my home?"

"Tarleton. Tarleton, Georgia."

Troy is obviously confused and finds this story utterly preposterous. "What could possibly have led you here?"

Jill smiles, "Surveys. That darn survey. You love to do surveys."

"Surveys? Odd...me?"

"Yeah. We were able to trace the survey to Erica, then to you."

"I don't understand any of this. Are you trying to tell me that Erica, my marriage...it's all a hoax?"

"Bingo."

"And she kidnapped me?"

"Yes."

"You and your daughter, my daughter...Madi...huh, you make great investigators. But why would Erica go through all of this?"

"Oh, I don't know. Who could explain her sick, twisted, and perverted mind? She's a monster."

Troy, filled with questions, anger, and distrust, looks at Jill. "This is a lot to take in."

"Unbelievable, I know. But I promise it's all true. And there's one more thing."

"Torture me more." Troy listens.

With tears in her eyes, "I'm your wife."

This disturbs him even more. He holds his head in his hand as if excruciating pain spears through one side of his forehead to the other. His fingers massage around his eyes to his temples, trying to ease what appears to be pain from the shock of what he's just learned. He looks straight ahead, then turns to Jill.

His white eyes penetrate her. Then he says, "I know."

She screams in fear and tries to escape kicking at the robotic double but he staves her off. She races for the door handle, but he quickly locks the doors.

With no one around to help in the middle of nowhere land, she tries to fight the ghost-eyed villainous fiend off. They struggle over the steering wheel as she grabs for it making the car swerve across the road, left to right, uncontrollably. The car slides over the icy median having near misses of hitting a tree and running over the bushes crushing them. The lookalike gains control and

Jill attempts to elbow him in the neck, but he blocks her strike. He backhands her hard and she collapses, knocked out. The double drives back down the road with Jill slumped back on the seat.

———— ∞∞ ————

MINUTES HAVE PASSED as the lookalike drives up to the front of the house. Jill is still unconscious. The double gets duct tape from the rear of the car and binds her hands at the wrist. He enters the house with her thrown over his shoulder. She comes to but does not stir while he carries her downstairs to a basement lab, a mini replica of a sophisticated technological lab. Jill looks around for something to help her escape. She studies the room. In a corner, there is a huge medical monitor resting on a wall and shelves lined with various books on medicine, psychology, neuroscience, computer cloning, and of course entomology sitting next to it. Bottles of chemicals cover another shelf and some sparingly scattered over a lab counter. Medical equipment—an IV and a monitor for the heart and body rate with strands of electrode wires hanging are stationed next to Troy lying unconscious on a cushioned metal gurney. He is strapped down at the wrists and ankles. Jill manages to wrestle out of the lookalike's arms and land on her feet. She pushes past the double, rushing over to Troy, affectionately circling his face with kisses. He comes out of his unconscious state.

"Troy, Troy, what have they done to you?"

Troy's reaction to Jill is one of evasion and surprise; he does not recognize nor understand her affectionate and attentive behavior toward him.

"Who are you? Am I supposed to know you?"

"I'm your w—," Jill anxious to respond is cut short.

"—you're nothing, nothing to him." Erica interrupts Jill before she can finish saying the word, wife as she comes down the stairs.

"What's the matter, Erica?" Jill counters. "Afraid he's going to find out the truth, that you're a psycho bitch?"

Troy affirms, "Too late, I've already discovered that."

Erica, feeling abandoned and betrayed by Troy, begs, "Don't say that. You don't mean it!"

He looks over at Jill, wondering how she fits in this mixed-up puzzle. What could this woman, another stranger to him, reveal that would make sense of this crazy scenario of events?

"Who are you?"

Jill asks, "Are you ready for another surprise?"

Troy looks at Jill with questioning eyes.

"Then brace yourself. I'm your wife."

"This is all so unbelievable," he says. The revelation learning that Erica has lied to him but another is his wife is too much to absorb. Another sharp pain spears through Troy's head. He cringes. "Make the pain go away."

"No more lies, Erica. Now he knows the truth."

Erica pushes Jill away from Troy. "Get away from him. You see, he doesn't believe your lies. And, your lies are hurting him."

"Ohhhhh," Troy moans. "Make the pain stop!"

Erica screams at the top of her lungs, insanely insisting that Jill is not his wife. Her symbolic source of release, a wooden chair, sits next to her. She begins to claw her nails into it, inflicting what one would think is horrific pain but she has become so numb to this and just adds to the wounded stripes already deeply set in. Tears slide down her cheeks from the disappointment and pain she's feeling in her heart, knowing that Troy will never love her. She lambasts the synthetic lookalike. "You were supposed to take care of her. Why didn't you kill her?"

While she has a tantrum, he tugs at the wrist and ankle restraints, trying to break loose. The restraints loosen some. Neither Erica nor the double notices the loosened chained ring that has slightly lifted from its socket in the wall.

Erica crosses over to a drawer in the lab and pulls out the small velvet-lined case. Jill has become all too familiar with its contents—two syringes lying side by side next to two vials. Erica fills each syringe. She squirts a little to test the flow.

"Remember this. One, for your memory. And you, my pretty nemesis, this one is for you. Finally, it's good-bye forever."

Jill boldly retorts, "You may have his mind, but you'll never have his heart."

Crazed with anger, Erica slaps Jill hard across the face, slicing her lip, while the double pins her arms back. Blood, the color of crimson, runs down the side of her chin from the split lip. "Is that your best shot?" Jill mocks.

Troy asks Erica to stop, and his concern for Jill only angers her more.

"I got rid of his past, and now I'll get rid of you forever, which should have been done a long time ago." She cuts her eyes over at the double for he did not complete what she had sent him to do earlier.

Erica filled with such intense hate raises the syringe high ready to inject her with the fatal solution. But before she can strike her, Jill headbutts Erica in the face hard, knocking her against the gurney Troy lies on, which slams him hard against the wall.

His head smashes into the wall, and a wrist restraint chained to the wall snaps free unnoticed by either Erica or the lookalike. The syringe is jolted out of Erica's hand and slides under the lab counter. Jill charges toward Erica again, head first, but the robot blocks her path stepping between them and backhands her across the room, banging her body and head against a metal table with surgical tools on it. She slides down to the floor, knocking some of the tools down, including a small scalpel which she grabs and conceals. She pretends to be unconscious.

Neither the double nor Erica notices Jill concealing the scalpel behind her. Now, sprawled out on the floor with her hands bound behind her and the scalpel between her fingers, she slowly maneuvers cutting the binding wrapped around her wrists.

The double motions toward Jill to finish her off, but Erica stops him.

"Leave her for now and help me with him. She's not going anywhere."

Troy's head painfully aches, and his vision is slightly blurred.

As a precaution, Erica fearful that Troy might regain his memory from the hard jolt against the wall attempts to take steps to ensure that does not happen. She is determined that his past is going to stay just that. She will give him one more injection of the memory-altering solution to ensure his past is gone forever. Erica commands the lookalike to push Troy over to her.

He pushes the gurney toward Erica, but when he passes in front of Jill, she jumps at him and stabs him in the back with the scalpel. He falters and stumbles from the slight aggravation, then pulls the scalpel out.

Jill pushes Troy out of the way and elbows the imposter several times in the face. She smashes his face very hard with her palm. He stumbles. Opportunity—Jill quickly dives over to the lab counter and grabs a bottle of acid. She douses him with it.

"Say goodbye." Jill torches him with a Bunsen burner that sits on the counter. The acid ignites and his synthetic skin melts like candle wax. Bit by bit, the melting skin drips to the floor, evaporating as quickly as it falls to the floor.

The moisture shorts some of his computer circuits, but before Jill can torch his entire body, Erica knocks the flame burner from her hands. The part metal skeleton and remains of the synthetic-skinned robot charges toward Jill like a vicious angry bull. He throws lab equipment aside and anything blocking his path to get to her. She backs up with every step he takes to try to get away.

The remains of this six-foot-four metal colossal leans down into Jill's face, eye to eye. Fury drives him, just like the sick mind that created him. His hand, partially covered with skin eaten and burned away from the acid and fire, grabs her throat gripping tighter and tighter. Strangling almost every ounce of life from her, he lifts Jill off the floor.

Troy regains his strength and frees himself from the other restraint. Quickly, he rushes over to rescue Jill and begins to fight the robotic monster, plowing his fists into his side multiple times, robot against human.

"Let her go!"

But his grip tightens around her neck.

"Let her go! You piece of scrap metal shit."

The replica's eyes turn white. He releases his fingers from Jill's neck and drops her listless body. She gasps for air struggling to breathe as she plummets to the floor next to the heart rate monitor.

"It's me you want, so let's finish this," Troy says.

They begin a karate sparring match, each blocking the other's advances. On Troy's fifth or sixth blow to the robot's body, the double blocks his fist and backhands him across the face multiple times. His backhands are so hard that every blow pushes Troy back, blow by blow and step by step. As the robot steps forward with each blow, blood splatters over Troy's face. Troy grabs a metal tube from the counter and whacks the robot across the head. The hit stuns him for a second but he is invincible.

Watching the double's merciless strikes on Troy's badly beaten face, Jill pulls up on the monitor stand and yanks an electrode wire from the monitor. She struggles crawling over to Troy and wraps the silicon-coated tubing around the robot's neck, twisting it tighter and tighter trying to destroy his computer system. Erica dives for the velvet box lying on the floor and lunges at Jill to stab her in the face, but she ducks and Erica misses. Then, Jill releases her grip on the robot and plows her foot into Erica with a hard side kick. Erica grabs her side and cringes in pain. She yells at Jill, "He belongs to me."

Troy collapses to his knees, badly beaten, bloody, and weak. His puffy eyes and bruised bloody face covered in red like the smoldering fire that surrounds them, looks up at the mechanical imposter. Fierce to the end, he says, "Make it good, 'cause this ends with you."

The robot's charred skeleton picks Troy's limp body up and lifts him over his head. He readies himself for the final kill to break Troy's spine.

"No stop! Don't hurt him. Put him down." Erica commands.

The robot ignores her commands and arches Troy's body a little, about to snap his back.

Jill watches, horrified, fearing the worst will happen to her love. "No!" She yells and looks for something to help him.

Erica commands her creation again, "Put him down."

He obeys and drops Troy hard on the floor who moans in pain.

Quickly, Jill dives for the other syringe lying on the floor next to the lab counter. Erica breaks the dive, choking her from behind, but not before Jill slyly rolls the syringe near Troy.

Erica whispers in Jill's ear, "Now to finish you off. You won't remember a thing. You'll never see your family again. Troy will eventually bring a new wife home, me, because you will have disappeared, having no memory of them. Then, what's her name…Madi, your daughter, will grow to love me, grow to know me as her sweet new mother."

"No, bitch," Jill gasps, "you're not Mommie Dearest."

She wraps her arms around Erica's neck and flips her over. She scrambles over to Troy and slides in, grabbing the syringe near Troy and tosses it to him.

He jabs the syringe through the robot's metal white eye, which leads to the main artery of his computer system. The fictitious replica crouches over, cringing as the solution runs through the tubes that gave him life. His virtual computer system shuts down, file after file. He grabs the syringe stuck in his eye and pulls it out, then collapses to the floor.

Erica yells, "It's not over! Truth is, I am his woman, and you will never take him away from me again." Erica belts Jill in the face several times with her fist, but Jill blocks her next hit and elbows her in the neck. Erica grabs her throat, gasping.

Jill leans into Erica's face, staring through her. "And truth hurts. I am his wife, his woman, the first and the last." Jill belts Erica hard in the face with her fist, knocking Erica out. She collapses to the floor unconscious.

Jill rushes over to Troy, who lies on the floor badly beaten. His eyes are shut closed. She cradles Troy's head on her lap. "Come on, baby! Come on. Stay with me. Stay with me! I love you. She cries out. "Live!"

His eyelids barely opened. "Jill…"

"You remember." Tears of joy fill her eyes.

He has a moment of instant replay that takes him back to the all-star basketball game, his friends, the shots that killed them, and the pool of blood they laid in. The pain in his temple shoots from the back of his head to the frontal lobe. He holds his head between his hands, closing his eyes to try to lessen the pain. Then he remembers the torture Erica has taken him through over the past weeks and months. His memory has come back. Rage infuriates him as he looks over at Erica.

"You did this to me. My friends, my family. What are you?"

Erica trying to offer some bit of redemption, "No, no, no. I'm sorry. Please forgive me. I would never hurt y…"

But, Troy interrupts her and turns to the only woman he knows and truly loves. "Jill, I love you. Let's get out of here." He dismisses Erica's plea and gives her apology no credence.

Suddenly, Erica lunges over to Jill with the fatal solution syringe to stab her.

"Oh, no you don't. Get away from him!"

She stabs at Jill several times, but Jill ducks and grabs a scalpel from the counter. She slashes Erica's arm, then stabs her in the chest. Blood seeps through her white lab coat, creating a red stain that spreads wider and wider as the blood rushes from her body. She falls on her face holding her chest and drops the syringe.

The lab is engulfed in flames quickly traveling around Erica, Troy, and Jill. Troy grabs Jill's hand. "Let's get out of here." Troy urges.

Jill grabs the gun that peeps out from her purse lying on the floor. She stuffs it in the back of her pants. Jill and Troy limp over to a window, his arm thrown over her shoulder. He grabs a chair and sails it through the window, shattering it.

As they exit through the window, Troy hears a shallow soft plea through the blazing fire. "Help, please help me!" Erica cries.

Troy grabs a blanket lying on the floor and wraps it around Jill. "Go, baby, go." Troy ushers Jill to the window. He helps her out to safety but he doesn't follow.

Jill looks back. "What are you doing?" she asks, frantically.

"I can't leave her."

Jill revisits the torture this woman has put them through. How she tried to kill her loved ones and her. The woman does not deserve this kind of loyalty, but she reconciles the fact that she married a good man, and after all, no matter how crazy the psycho bitch is, she is human.

Erica surrounded in fire looks up at the blazing ceiling and cries out, "My babies!" The living room above is engulfed in flames. The aquarium glass shatters and inside, the albino scorpions shrivel up as the fire burns them.

Erica cries out again, "Help, please help!"

"Go!" Troy insists. He helps Jill through the window. Her heart breaks with concern for him. "Not without you." Erica's fingers crawl to the syringe lying on the floor and with one last effort, she bursts through the flames, charging over to Troy with the syringe. "And not without me!" she screams.

"This is my family, and I want it back." Jill fires several shots, emptying the gun's bullet chamber into Erica—four bullets, one in her arm, one in her side, one in the leg, and one in the chest. Erica collapses to the floor, blood spurting profusely from each opening and dripping from the corner of her mouth.

Finally, their nightmare, the torment, and this madness had come to an end. Troy climbs through the window, but all is not over. The metal hand of the robot grabs Troy's ankle, gripping tight, and pulls Troy back into the fiery house.

"AUTOMATIC RESET COMPLETE" flashes in the robotic lookalike's virtual screen. Troy twists and stomps at the metallic monster, trying unsuccessfully to break loose.

"Troy!" Jill calls out knowing that he was right behind her but cannot see him through the fire and smoke surrounding the house. She sees the white skin of his leg coming through the black smoke. Then the rest of the body, the white eyes of the tall metal skeleton, charges with fury through the black smoke toward her. She screams, "No! No!" then she runs.

But just as quickly as he takes off after her, a metal shaft rams into the back of the robot's head through his central computer system.

Troy stands at the end of the shaft, stabbing his nemesis. "That's my wife and this is your end."

The robot turns to Troy and slowly steps toward him. Troy backs away as the double stretches, reaching for Troy's neck. His hand wraps around Troy's neck, about to squeeze, but he freezes and collapses.

Parts of the burning house collapse to the ground behind Troy. He shoves the metal carcass into the fire with his foot. Exhausted and overcome by fire and smoke, he stumbles over to Jill. They embrace.

Chapter 30

FINALE

TROY AND JILL hold each other up, standing at a distance from the house and watching the smoldering fire take control of the house. As the burning house starts to collapse, so does the end of their nightmare. Tears roll down Jill's cheeks. She rests her head on his shoulder, and a feeling of peace envelopes her. "Finally, it's over," she says.

Troy hugs Jill very tight. It's as if he is so afraid that if he lets go, he'd lose her again. He moves his lips to hers and presses so tightly, parting them as he slides his tongue deep in her mouth, an exchange that she returns. She pulls him in closer, holding him and loving him back. She is, after all, the love he missed, the love he cherishes, the love of his life.

He says, "I love you. Let's go home."

And just as quickly as she feels the comfort of love and peace, worry takes over, thinking about what will happen to Troy with the impending legal issues facing him. But for now, her worries seem futile. She lifts her head from Troy's shoulder. He wipes the tears sliding down her face.

She barely gets a glimpse of a dark shadow darting from the burning house into the woods.

"Did you see that?" she asks.

"See what?"

"I thought I saw something over there, running from the house."

Troy looks toward the burning house as the blackened shell crumbles to the ground in the middle of the blazing fire and black smoke. "Your nerves, baby, just your nerves. Nothing could survive that."

Troy and Jill embrace again.

DEAD BRANCHES CRACKLE underneath the leaves and brush lying on the ground as footsteps rush over them. Two security agents, a male and female dressed in black suits and black shades, race ahead of the lookalike's charred metal skeleton carrying Erica's dangling bloody and burned body. Blood drips down her arm. The male agent calls out to the robot, "Hurry, the helicopter is just over the hill. We've got to get her to the lab quickly."

"If she survives," the other agent comments. She speaks through her wristband communicator. "Our ETA is two seconds. I repeat, two seconds."

As they come to a clearing at the end of the trail, they follow a whirlwind of debris and leaves being hurled by the rotating blades from the helicopter they approach. The terrorist Azra, wearing his signature red eye patch, comes up to the helicopter door leaning on it with his prosthetic hand. He looks down at Erica's blood-soaked and bruised unconscious body cradled in the robot's arms.

As the helicopter idles, the sound almost drowns out his anger. But the fierceness of his anger and disgust prevails. Azra yells, "He ruined my life. He took everything from me, and you failed."

He relives the day in Ogdaius when he lay on a ledge next to the fire, missing it by a hair and not close enough to burn him. Somewhat groggy from the fall, he lifted his bruised and bloody body to see his wife through a big opening of crumbled debris fall to her death.

He cried out, "Hanan!" Then heard a loud thump as her body hit the ground hard, twisted in her blood. Devastated and consumed with loss, the sound of a crying baby, his daughter, broke his grief. His eyes followed her cries traveling up to see his daughter about to experience the same fate as his wife, but the fall was broken by Troy. He hooked his hand in the swaddling wrapped around her body and pulled her to safety. He cradled her in his arms and called her, Madi. They fled across the rooftop, and Azra passed out.

The mewled sound of that painful memory fades back to the present moment. Erica's eyes pop open as her frail body, covered in crimson, is lifted onto the helicopter. Azra disappointed, haunted with hurt and hate, looks down on her. He angrily spurts out.

"Love has no ending. My obsession will see revenge."

THE END

About the Author

M. Réshor is a filmmaker, writer, and producer currently residing on the West Coast. Inspired by a background working in the world of information technology, this first novel, *Love Has No Ending*—a high-tech, intriguing story of obsession is set to be the first of a three-novel trilogy.